When The Flowers Breathe

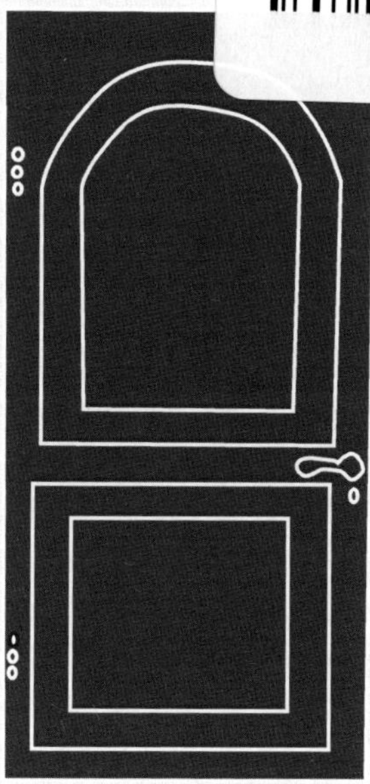

Red Rook Press

This is a work of fiction. Names, characters, and incidents either are the product of the author's imagination or are used fictitiously. Any resemblance to actual persons, living or dead, events, or locales is entirely coincidental.

To request permissions, contact the publisher at redrookpress@gmail.com.

Paperback: 979-8-9879562-6-7
Ebook: 979-8-9879562-2-9

Second paperback edition April 2024
Cover design: DeAndra Gauntt
artwork: Anat Melenteyv (*When the Flowers Breathe*),
Anna Luis (contents and short stories),
Michael Esparza ("Off the Page" and "Mocktails")

Printed by Mixam in the United States of America.

Red Rook Press
Box 870244
The University of Alabama
Tuscaloosa, AL 35487-0244

redrookpress.org

When The Flowers Breathe

Attalea Rose

Table of Contents

WHEN THE FLOWERS BREATHE

Special Edition

When the Flowers Breathe 7

NEW STORIES

Knowing 166

Jump 176

The Thunder 194

BEHIND THE SCENES

Off Page with Attalea Rose 224

BOOKCLUB

Mocktails 228

Discussion Questions 233

Acknowledgements 234

For my parents, Gordon and Theresa.

Welcome

1

I

New York City, March 2022

Alice Douglas perched at the edge of the sidewalk with her heels pressed together, a kitchen knife and an opened letter tucked in the pocket of her rosebud-pink peacoat. Her toes hung over the edge of the curb, her heels keeping her grounded to the concrete, and her strawberry-blonde hair floated loosely around her shoulders. She kept gliding her fingertips against the crown of her head, pushing the locks away from her forehead, fighting against the breeze kicked up from iconic yellow taxicabs and cars with illegally tinted windows to keep her hair out of her eyes.

Across the street from Alice, tucked between a drugstore and a dark alley, was Tranquility. The flashing red-neon sign cast a warm glow over the exposed alabaster freckle-speckled skin of Alice's face and hands. She'd walked past the storefront, the same stilted alley—it wasn't too far away from Barnard, where she went to college—many times, traversing the bustling Manhattan streets in search of coffee shops and thrift stores, yet she couldn't recall seeing the Tranquility before.

Alice walked to, then waited, at a crosswalk. Even when she had the illuminated, yellow-green pedestrian walk sign, she looked both ways, her head swiveling rapidly like a pent-up bobblehead finally released, before darting across the road in the designated gap in traffic. Her kitten-heeled black boots clicked against the concrete.

Alice could smell Tranquility before her hand reached the doorknob. A heady cloud of vanilla, lavender, and balsam perfume permeated through the frosted front window, through seams around the crimson-red-painted front door, and through the oakwood siding. Alice's nostrils flared, being assailed by scent so suddenly. She shuddered, and her peacoat quivered. The knife and letter in her pocket bounced twice off her thigh.

Alice looped her fingers around the doorknob—which, upon closer inspection was ornately engraved with a curled-up toad—and pulled open the door.

Stepping over the threshold was sauntering into wonderland. The lighting was hazy, and a slim layer of fog obscured Alice's peripheral vision. As she flailed her head like a biting dog thrashing against a muzzle, the fog shifted to remain in the edges of her sight, creating a stifling tunnel vision, like carriage horses wearing blinders. Alice thrust her hands into her pockets, one hand wrapping tentatively around the handle of the knife, took a shaky deep breath, and slowly surveyed her surroundings.

Alice was in a waiting room of sorts. There was a pink-velvet plush couch and three rocking chairs nestled beneath the front window, which gave a crystal-clear view out onto the street and the cars blurring past. An unattended reception desk made from spruce wood was tucked against the far wall. Beneath Alice's kitten-heeled boots were white tiles with blue grout.

"Can I help you?"

Alice whirled in a quick, tight circle, fog following her still. There was no one in the room besides her. Her hand tightened on the knife.

"Blink a couple times for me, dear." Alice complied without thinking, blinking rapidly, eyelashes fluttering like a drowning butterfly's wings. Then, there, behind the reception desk was a lean man with dark hair graying at his temples. He wore wired spectacles and a pressed, blue-wool suit with a red tie. "What can I do for you?" the man asked.

Alice approached the desk, her kitten-heels scuffing against the white-ceramic tiles. She pushed her hair behind her ears with the hand not clutching the knife handle. Alice cleared her throat and said, "My aunt invited me to come visit her, here."

The man ducked behind the desk, bent over at the waist, then emerged with a thick tome. It had a smooth, scuffed, brown-leather cover and at least a thousand pages. He set it atop the reception desk, which was cluttered with vibrant flower petals, three tawny quills, and four glass bottles of ink. "What is your aunt's name?"

"Lilith Hubbard."

The man stilled, his hands poised above the book, just about to flip it open. "You must be Alice, then. She said you might be coming. We hoped you would." A little bit of the tight ball in Alice's stomach loosened and she let go of the knife, letting it settle back into her pocket. She was in the right place, after all. "Well, we'll just get you all checked in, and then off to your Aunt Lilith."

"Thank you."

The man opened the tome, then tapped one of the quills into an inkwell. "What does the air smell like?" he said.

"Excuse me?"

"What does the air smell like?" the man repeated, quill poised over a half-filled page.

"Um . . ." Alice said slowly, "vanilla, lavender, and a Christmas tree."

He scribbled in a single line across a page. "Interesting. I've heard vanilla quite a bit, lavender, too, but the Christmas tree? That's interesting." He set his quill down, blew on the wet page to hasten the drying process, and after testing the newly written words with his forefinger, slammed the book closed.

"To me," the man continued, "I've always smelled frosted sugar cookies and the dried sea salt left on my skin from swimming in the Pacific Ocean as a kid. Makes me perpetually cold, thinking about it." He shuddered for emphasis. "I'm Robin," he introduced. His brows knit together as he asked, "I don't suppose your aunt has mentioned me at all . . .?" Alice shook her head, mouth drawn down for sympathy's sake. "Then you'll have to take my word that Lilith and I are old friends. She'll be so happy you're here."

"I hope so."

"I know so! I can't leave the front desk, so you'll have to go find her on your own. She's just through that door there." Robin pointed to a crimson-red door—nearly identical to the front door, except rather than a frog-engraved handle, this door had a curved swan's head for a doorknob—that Alice undoubtedly did not see before.

"Thank you, Robin," Alice murmured.

"You're very welcome."

As Alice approached the door, the fogginess in her peripheral vision faded, and she could see the room as it fully was: an interestingly furnished waiting room with walls covered in paintings of butterflies and moths, and Robin reading a heavily-creased copy of *Pride and Prejudice* from behind a reception desk. Alice pulled the door open, and as she stepped through it, a woman from outside walked past the front window. Alice could have sworn she had dove wings protruding from her shoulder blades.

2

New York City, March 2022

The newly appeared red door led to a dimly lit, stubby hallway with a gauzy, baby-pink curtain draped across the other end. Alice shuffled through the hallway, her right hand pressed against the wall, until she was shoving the curtain aside and walking into a speakeasy of sorts.

The lighting of the room was directed toward a broad stage against the far wall, with thick red-velvet curtains parted down the middle and a singer center-stage, leaning into a microphone on a stand as he sung a melancholy ballad. The rest of the room was dimly lit by sconces mounted on the walls and flickering, white-wax candles on creamy-white tableclothed tabletops. Every table was full, with guests in evening dresses and brightly colored suits reclining in plush chairs. They dined on plates of smoked salmon or medium-rare steak or heavily dressed Caesar salads, watching the singer as he bellowed into the microphone. The singer wore a plum-purple suit, and his hair was silvery-gray.

Alice felt underdressed in her peacoat, failing at obscuring her vintage Strawberry Shortcake graphic T-shirt and baggy, distressed jeans.

Adjacent to the stage was a bar, with circular barstools, also nearly full, wrapped around it. There were two bartenders, one elaborately twirling glass bottles in the air and the other watching in awe as a customer kept waving to get his attention. Along the perimeter of the room, beneath the sconces, were red-velvet couches and spruce wood coffee tables, also full of patrons sipping on champagne, talking amongst themselves softly.

Not spotting Aunt Lilith among the guests and unsure where to search next, Alice figured the bar was a good place to start, especially as it was the only available seating. Alice reached into her pocket, nudged aside the knife, and pulled the opened letter out of her pocket. She clenched the envelope tightly between her fingertips, wrinkling the paper, and approached one of the few empty seats at the bar. She pressed her free hand flat against the counter and said, "Excuse me?" just loud enough to get a bartender's attention.

The previously awe-struck bartender hurried over, having been scowled at by the juggling bartender for not attending to the customers. He wore a white button-down, the sleeves rolled up to his elbows, with a black vest and black tie, his collar popped in the back and tight blond curls that stuck out in every which direction.

"What can I get for you?" he asked.

Alice was still standing, and she leaned closer to the bartender, the edge of the counter digging into the bottom of her ribcage through her peacoat. "I'm looking for Lilith Hubbard?"

"Lilith should be backstage, she's on next—" Cue another dirty look from the other bartender "—but, uh . . . Customers aren't allowed backstage, so just take a seat and you can wave her over after her set."

"Her set?" Alice asked as she slid onto the barstool and faced the stage.

"First time here?"

"Yes," Alice whispered. She fiddled with the corner of the letter, swaying the paper back and forth beneath her thumb.

"Just a moment," he said, reaching behind the bar for a clean glass and a bottle of amber liquid. As he poured the drink into the champagne flute, it turned bright, high-carotene-flamingo pink and started fizzing, then he dropped a maraschino cherry into the glass with a *plink*. "Here." He pushed the glass across the bar toward Alice. His fingernails were stubby and painted midnight blue. "Non-alcoholic, on the house, a welcome drink."

Alice smiled with her lips but not her eyes and wrapped the fingers of her left hand around the glass stem, her right hand still clutching her letter. "Thank you."

The singer onstage finished his ballad, and the patrons clapped riotously, some whooping and hollering. He bowed a couple times and backed away from the microphone, until an unseen announcer said, "We now welcome to the stage, Miss Lilith Hubbard."

Alice let go of the drink, shoved her letter back in her pocket, swiveled in her seat, and leaned forward, her nose pushed as close to the stage as she could without toppling off her barstool. There was her Aunt Lilith, gliding onto the stage in a floor-length, long-sleeved, backless, royal purple gown. As Lilith passed the other singer, they gave one another a side hug, then Aunt Lilith was standing in front of the microphone.

Lilith was simultaneously exactly like and the opposite of how Alice envisioned her aunt. Whenever Aunt Lilith had come to visit, years ago, Aunt Lilith had been a coveralls sort, with calloused palms and heavy work boots. But Aunt Lilith could also be mended bird wings and eyeliner, bedazzled T-shirts and glittery arts and crafts.

"Thank you all for coming out tonight," Lilith said in her concise, clear, albeit clipped way of talking. The perfect balance between sultry and monotone. "I'll be finishing out the night with a composition by none other than our very own Mateo Cruz." She gestured to the bar, where the bottle-twirler was flushing and giving the crowd a half bow amidst applause. "This is 'Knowing.'"

A soundtrack crackled to life for three bars, then Aunt Lilith began softly singing a haunting, minor-key harmony. The crowd—and Alice—were riveted, watching the way Lilith's red lipsticked lips formed vowels and how her hand gently clutched the microphone.

"Have you ever heard her sing before?" the bartender, the one who gave Alice the drink, asked. The other customers at the bar weren't ordering drinks, instead focused on Lilith.

"I thought I had," Alice replied, forcing herself to sit up straight and lean an elbow against the bar. She nudged her still-full drink aside accidentally, and her sleeve soaked up condensation from the glass. Alice filtered through memories of Aunt Lilith, of Aunt Lilith singing lullabies before nap times, but Alice couldn't remember the timber of Aunt Lilith's voice. "Admittedly, I guess I haven't."

"Lilith doesn't always sing. I'm glad you were able to catch her tonight."

Alice swiveled in her barstool, her body now facing the bartender. "What is this place?"

"Tranquility?"

"Yes. Is it a bar? A theater?"

The bartender put a hand on one hip, then splayed out the fingers of his other hand and said in a high-pitched voice, "'You're using mundane words to describe the extraordinary.'" Alice's brow knit, then he crossed his arms and sheepishly said, "Well, that's what Lilith always says anyways."

"How long have you worked here, Mister . . ." Alice scanned the bartender's lapel for a nametag, but there wasn't one.

"Vincent, and I've worked here . . ." Vincent tapped his pointer finger on his opposite pinkie. "A half a year now. Huh. How about that. Where do you hail from, Miss . . ."

"I'm Alice. I'm Lilith's niece."

Vincent's eyebrows raised. "Niece? I didn't know Lilith had any family beyond us." Alice's gaze dropped and she began drawing lines in the condensation on her glass with her fingers. "Not that you aren't important to her!" Vincent tried to backpedal. "Lilith is pretty private about her life. Not that any of us blame her."

The soundtrack swelled a few notches louder, then Lilith belted out a high A, and the crowd erupted into applause. "Now's your chance," Vincent urged. "Since Lilith's your aunt, then you're probably—" he dropped his voice to a hushed whisper and side-eyed the other bartender, "—fine going backstage. There's a staircase and a door to the right of the stage, you'll find her through there."

"Thank you," Alice whispered, hopping off her stool. She took one step toward the stage, then reached back for her untouched drink. She took one sip, and her mouth filled with liquid strawberry tart and fizzy bubbles.

3

New York City, March 2022

Backstage was cramped. It wasn't terribly small, granted, but it was cluttered with racks of costumes and two rows of vanities. It was sparsely illuminated by bulbous vanity lights embedded around the vanity mirrors, and remnants of the stage lights crept through the seams of the now-closed velvet curtains.

In the gaps between the clutter, Alice could see four people backstage, lounging in the back corner on two matching, plush, orange-leather couches and sipping on flutes of champagne. They were laughing, partially dressed in formalwear yet draped in blankets and sweatshirts.

"—way he looks at her," one of them was saying, the singer that had performed right before Lilith, "he is entirely too obvious! If I were him, I'd work up the gumption to just ask her out—"

"We all know how much gumption you have," another teased, a willowy woman with tightly curled hair and brown skin.

The singer pouted. "Well, maybe not back in the day but—"

"Alice?" The conversation halted, and there was Lilith, standing. She was still in her royal purple gown, and as she stood, a wool, gray blanket drifted to the floor. Her hair, the same strawberry blonde as Alice's, drifted in an unseen breeze to her waist. Lilith's three companions followed Lilith's gaze to latch onto Alice in her peacoat and her flushed, freckled cheeks.

Alice reached into her pocket and pulled out the crinkled letter. "Um, I got your letter?" Alice said. Her voice pinged off the vanity mirrors for an uncomfortable three seconds as the other singers exchanged surprised whispers.

"Wonderful!" Lilith beamed. She beckoned Alice closer with her fingers. Alice wove through the maze of clothes and vanities, and as soon as she was within range of Lilith's arm span, Lilith wrapped Alice in a brittle hug and said to the others, "This is my niece, Alice."

There was a chorus of "Niece?" "I didn't know you had a niece!" and "She's gorgeous, it clearly runs in the family!" from the singers.

"Yes, I have a niece! She'll be staying with us this week for her spring break." Lilith raised an eyebrow. "If she would like to?"

"Yes," Alice replied, some of the tension leeching from her shoulders.

"Alice, these are the singers, Josiah, Enid, and Carmela." Lilith motioned to the assortment of people on the couch with a swooping hand. "And there's one more, Max, but they're not here tonight. You'll meet them soon." The three singers waved, but Lilith was tugging Alice away before further introductions could be made. "Come, let's get you settled. You'll have plenty of time to make friends later."

A, "Sleep well, honey!" from Carmela plinked against Alice's back as she walked away. Lilith led Alice back into the main room, past the customers at their tables and couches—Lilith waved and winked all the while—then back into that stumpy little dark hallway from earlier, except this time, there was a glinting gold handle in the wall, revealing yet another not-there-before but suddenly-here-now door, this one with a gold, koi-fish doorknob.

Through that door they went, Lilith ushering Alice in first, through a tight doorway. It led to a new hallway, a longer one, brightly lit with brass sconces, and this hallway was full of doors, at least ten of them, each painted a different color, emerald green and blood red and royal blue and coral pink. There were live flowers growing from the walls, vines of white orchids, yellow chrysanthemums, crimson dahlias, and black calla lilies. As they walked, the open blooms continually faced Lilith and Alice, and they bounced in tune with their footsteps.

Lilith pointed at one of the last doors in the hallway, to the right, painted a baby blue, and motioned for Alice to open it. It was a bedroom, with cream walls, a four-poster black metal bedframe with a blue-paisley bedspread and tasseled decorative pillows, a low dresser beneath a window draped in gauzy off-white lace curtains, and a short bookshelf that served as a nightstand.

"You'll be here, then," Lilith said, flicking on the overhead light. "There are fresh towels and soap in the ensuite." She pointed to a slim door near the dresser, which presumably led to the bathroom.

Alice was ogling the room, comparing its quaint decoration to the desolate dorm room she had become accustomed to over the past year.

"So, I can really stay?" Alice asked slowly.

"Of course, was that not already established?"

"Not entirely." Alice pinched the letter between her fingers again, remembering the crisp handwriting of her aunt.

"I apologize. Logistics are more Robin's thing than mine."

The letter arrived three weeks ago at the mail center at Barnard. Alice was in her sophomore year there, and she stopped by in the hopes that a love letter would be waiting for her, but instead she found the letter from Lilith. The letter was curious, with a wax seal and decorated in Lilith's distinctive loopy handwriting. Within was a single slip of paper which read, *"Dearest Alice, I've heard from my sister that you're in the throes of heartache right now—I'd like to invite you to spend your spring break with me, at Tranquility. Protect yourself until I see you. Love, Aunt Lilith."* On the back of the paper was a map with a red circle around Tranquility.

Alice had written back, asking logistical questions about arrival and departure times, when and what to tell her mother, whether to expect New York City sightseeing or pajama days binge-watching TV shows, but Lilith never replied. And Alice couldn't text or call—Aunt Lilith didn't believe in cell phones, and if she had a landline, Alice didn't know the number. Lilith liked to be the one to reach out, not the one to be reached out to.

But, despite not knowing what to expect, Alice canceled her plane tickets home. Told her roommate she was spending spring break with her aunt. Her dorm building was open all week, so if the planned Tranquility vacation fell through, Alice would still have somewhere to stay.

"I really don't want to go back home right now," Alice confessed to her aunt.

"I understand," Lilith sighed. "My sister really is not the best when it comes to words of comfort." She winked at Alice. "If there's one thing you'll learn before you head back to school is that here, we're big on words. And emotions. There'll be no lack of support here."

"Thank you, Aunt Lilith." And Alice was grateful, truly.

"Let's get you settled! Did you not bring a bag?"

"No, I thought I'd see you first. I can go back to my dorm and get a few things tomorrow."

"There should be a cozy shirt or two in the dresser, that should get you through tonight." Lilith reached to take Alice's peacoat as Alice shrugged it off.

"Oh, watch out!" Alice cried, making Lilith halt with her hands fisted in the coat. "There's a knife in the pocket."

Lilith reached into the heavy pocket carefully and pulled out the kitchen knife. It was serrated and had a plastic sheath. "Why do you have this in your pocket?"

"Your letter said to protect myself!"

Lilith threw her head back and laughed. "I was talking metaphorically!" Alice frowned, deeper and deeper, as her aunt laughed harder. "I don't mean to mock you," she said between subsiding laughter,

"I'm not mocking you. I think you're a bright young woman."

"Aunt Lilith, why did you invite me? What is this place?"

Lilith set the peacoat over the bedframe and the knife on the bookshelf-nightstand, then plopped down on the bed and patted beside her with her palm. Alice sat down, and Lilith draped an arm over her shoulder, her tulle gown sleeves scratching against the bare skin of Alice's arms.

"I'm sorry, my dear, I don't mean to be cryptic." Lilith tapped her chin with an index finger. "Well, never mind, I most definitely do. I sent you the letter because I think this place can help you. Your mom told me that you seemed lost right now, and I think you spending spring break here with me will be healthier for you and more ideal for your mom."

Alice shook her head and stared at her hands. She opened her mouth to say something, then pressed her lips together and shook her head again.

"Tranquility is a place for the once displaced," Lilith continued. "Each one of us here has had our heart broken, then stitched back together again. While you're here, ask questions, then listen, then reflect. And take time to process your emotions amidst learning about the emotions of others. Does that make a little more sense?"

"Yes." Alice picked at her thumb, nursing a thin slab of loose skin. "Is Tranquility a restaurant? Or a nightclub?"

"It's . . . I guess you would say a theater." Lilith made a disgruntled noise in the back of her throat and scowled. "Tranquility doesn't really have a definition. It is what it is."

"But how do you stay in business? What about rent and food and . . . and taxes?"

Lilith waved a hand in the air. "Oh, those are worldly things. We don't worry about those here."

"Okay." Alice was staring at the floor, at the hardwood floors. They were marbled with tree rings, and Alice counted the dark lines as they rippled across the floor. Her temples pulsed with an emerging headache.

Lilith grabbed Alice by the shoulders and rocked her side to side playfully, gently. "Stop worrying about logistics. You're on vacation now, you're here with your dear old aunt, it's been a couple years since I've seen you, we're all going to have a grand time."

"Thank you, Aunt Lilith."

"Of course, dear." Lilith squeezed Alice's shoulder once, then stood, walked toward the door. Stopped with her hand resting on the frame. "I was nineteen and brokenhearted, too, once," Lilith said.

Alice ground the palm of her hand into her eye socket. "And you lived, and I'll live through it, too, I know. Mom keeps telling me that."

"Oh, no, I was going to say it was one of the hardest things I've ever had to go through, being heartbroken at nineteen."

"Really?"

"Yes. I remember not thinking I'd live through it, but everyone around me telling me I would, and that I was being dramatic." Lilith fluffed up her hair, scratching her scalp with shaped nails. "With age, people can forget what it was like to be young, young and in love, young and terrified. I've tried not to be one of those people." Lilith sighed wistfully and settled back down on the bed. "His name was Arnold. Would you like to know the full story of my First Great Heartbreak?"

The Douglas family was a private one. They didn't talk about the drama of the past, about previous boyfriends and girlfriends, about being young and in love. Aunt Lilith was presenting Alice with the taboo. What else could Alice say except, "Yes."

4

CLEVELAND, OHIO MARCH 1992

When Arnold Harrison's best friend, James Douglas, said, "If you take Lilith, I can take Ellie," Arnold felt as if his lungs had just been crushed in a trash compactor rife with three-day old rotting banana peels.

"No," Arnold hissed, taking a dramatic bite from his fluffernutter sandwich and staring pointedly at the cafeteria wall and its, *"Reduce, reuse, recycle!"* mural over James' shoulder.

"Please?" James asked. He pushed his dark hair off his forehead, then squeezed his scalp with his fingers. There were bags under his bloodshot eyes and pink glitter under his fingernails.

"I don't know," Arnold grumbled, but the truth was, he knew this was a big deal. James had never been this smitten with a girl before. Finding the perfect way to ask Ellie to prom had been the only thing on James' mind for the past two weeks, even taking precedent over his chemistry final—which he aced anyways, though barely an A, almost an A minus.

"I'll owe you big time."

"You'll owe me for life!" Arnold took another bite of his fluffernutter and pushed his wiry glasses up his nose. For as blatantly obvious as James' infatuation with Ellie was, Arnold's hate toward Lilith was just as, if not more, obvious. It all started in the third grade, when Lilith stole his fluffernutter sandwich during lunch, took one bite, left a lopsided bite-mark from a missing front tooth, promptly announced it was the most disgusting thing she'd ever tasted, then handed it back and wailed at the top of her lungs until he'd gotten her an apple from the hot lunch line.

It was all downhill from there. Their last names were too close together, Harrison and Hubbard, that in their shared classes in middle school and high school, they were frequently stuck together for group projects. Lilith was demanding and bossy and wanted to run the show, something Arnold couldn't let her do. Their projects always ended in A's and bickering.

And now. *Now* Lilith was going to be valedictorian. They announced it last week. She'd beaten him by one lousy A in gym class while he'd only gotten a B plus. When they graduated in less than two months, he'd have to be the salutatorian to her valedictorian. Arnold couldn't imagine a more humiliating way to end his high school career.

"Look, I know my timing with this request is . . . not the best," James continued, "but this is my one shot. Please, can you just help me?"

Arnold sighed and dramatically stuffed the remaining half of his sandwich back into its Ziploc bag, suddenly no longer hungry. "This is romcom shit, you realize that, right?"

"Ellie loves romcoms," James sighed, all heart-eyed and mushy. He cleared his throat and shook his head. "She's already been asked to prom by three other guys, and she told them the same thing. Whoever can get someone to take Lilith, she'll go with them."

"Then Ellie is not worth it. Let one of the other guys take her." With the way James' eyes widened and his lips started frowning into a childish pout, Arnold knew there was no winning this argument. "Fine. I will ask Lilith. But I can't control whether she says yes or not."

James devolved into a droopy-shouldered, clasped-hands puddle of gratitude just as the bell rang. Arnold wasn't holding out hope for James. There was no way in hell Lilith would say yes to going to prom with him.

"Okay, sure," Lilith said. She was applying coral, sparkly lip gloss, staring at herself in the magnetic mirror of her locker door.

"What?" Arnold's stomach hardened, like a timelapse video of lava cooling to magma. He clutched his biology textbook and notebook in his hands. "You . . . *will?*"

"You're asking for your friend James, yes?" Lilith wasn't looking at him, still focused on her half-puckered lips and the glittery gloss.

"Yes."

"Then, yea, I'll go with you. I like James for Ellie."

"Oh." Arnold's lip curled, and Lilith caught the gesture in his reflection in her mirror.

"I'll be wearing midnight blue. Come pick me up when James picks up Ellie," Lilith said. She popped her lips together, tucked her lip gloss into her locker, then slammed the door closed. "Don't worry about a corsage, I can take care of that."

"Oh. Okay then."

5

CLEVELAND, OHIO MARCH 1992

"Why did she say yes?" Arnold griped for the third time that evening. They were in James' bedroom. Arnold was lying on his back on James' bed, his tie loosened, and the first few buttons of his crisp white dress shirt undone. His suit jacket was draped over the back of James' desk chair. The white of his shirt contrasted attractively with his umber skin tone, and he was wearing a navy-blue tie that complemented his eyes.

"Arnie, my man, you're pathetic," James said distractedly from where he stood in front of a full-body mirror hung on the closet doors. He frantically rotated through a series of three nearly identical ties, his arms pumping robotically like a bendable Barbie doll subject to a young child's curious whims. The ties were rose pink, to match Ellie's dress, one with thin white stripes, one with tiny white polka dots, and one solid colored.

James' bedroom was a converted attic, complete with the pointed roof and cliché circular window that looked out over the garage. It had beige carpet and beige walls, and if James' mother hadn't intercepted, James would have had beige furniture as well, but instead opted for a sleek, matching mahogany bedframe, bookshelf, nightstand, and desk set. Hung on the walls were superhero posters of any and every superhero imaginable, with crisp corners and sun faded artwork. James' favorite posters were the knockoffs, the parodies, with Bluebird instead of Robin, Manbat instead of Batman, and Powerfulman instead of Superman.

"I mean, she hates me," Arnold continued, "I hate her. Wouldn't—"

"Stop it." James settled on the tie with the thin white stripes and began knotting it together. "When we get to the dance, try not to bail within the first hour."

"No promises."

Suit jackets on, dress shirts buttoned, and ties tied, James and Arnold drove separately—Arnold wanted as quick an escape as possible, while James wanted to dance the night away—to Ellie and Lilith's house. They lived in a standard middle-class suburb, in a mundane house with white siding and a red front door. The family's two sedans were stacked in the house's two-car garage. Spindly branches of winterized shrubs lined the front walkway, and singular battery-operated candles flickered in the windows.

James and Arnold's dress shoes, severely lacking in traction, crunched against the remaining patches of spring snow that had drifted onto the previously shoveled walkway. James used the silver doorknocker, Arnold hiding behind him, then clutched the plastic container holding the corsage he'd bought for Ellie, with its lush, pink-veined lilies. James' breathing was clipped while Arnold took deep breaths.

Mrs. Hubbard answered the door. She was wearing a black T-shirt and jeans, with a digital camera in her hand. "Come in, come in!" she said, holding open the door with her foot and motioning the boys in with her free hand. "The girls are upstairs waiting to have a grand entrance."

The entryway was lit by a silver chandelier that hung from a vaulted ceiling. To the left was a sitting room, and to the right was the kitchen. Straight ahead a hallway beneath a swooping oakwood staircase with a cream carpet runner. The home smelled of freshly baked chocolate chip cookies.

The perfunctory sound of slammed doors trickled down the staircase, and Mrs. Hubbard whispered, "They heard the doorknocker." She raised her shoulders and let out a quick, excited, schoolgirl giggle. "They'll give it another minute or so, then come down." She took a few steps backward, leaving James and Arnold to stand directly beneath the chandelier, and raised her camera to wait.

James and Arnold's stomachs were each in knots. James' because the possible love of his life was about to walk down those stairs, Arnold's because his nemesis was about to walk down those stairs. The waiting was the hardest part.

And then they appeared, at the top of the stairs. Their strawberry blonde hair was drawn up in pinned updos, heavily hair sprayed into place. Lilith nudged Ellie to descend first, and she did, gliding down the stairs in her pink, lace-bodice, puffed sleeved ballgown, the hem draping against the stairs and the tips of her gold-sparkled shoes peeking out as she lifted the skirt to avoid tripping. James audibly gasped. The camera shutter clicked away.

James offered up his corsage, and the pinning process of his boutonniere began, while Lilith skipped down the stairs. She was in midnight blue, just as she'd told Arnold. The bodice had a scooped neckline and thin straps, and the dress was tight through her hips. Arnold couldn't look at her.

At the bottom of the stairs, Lilith sidestepped Ellie and James to reach Arnold. The camera shutter continued clicking, and Lilith shielded her face with a cupped hand and whispered, "Mom!" Lilith was already wearing a corsage of ocean-at-night blue roses around the wrist of the hand she'd raised, and in the other hand, she held out a matching boutonniere to Arnold.

"I didn't know roses came in blue," Arnold said. He wouldn't make eye contact with Lilith as she pinned it to his lapel.

"Not naturally," Lilith hummed.

"Let's get photos!" Mrs. Hubbard said, ushering the four into a group photo. James not-so-subtly wiped his clammy palms on his dress pants, then draped his arm around Ellie's shoulders. Arnold was a good foot away from Lilith. "Closer!" Arnold complied. He rested a hand against Lilith's waist. The fabric was softer than he was expecting, more of a caress than the unwelcoming, scratchy, cheap material he was expecting. "Okay, just the couples now,"

James and Ellie were first, making faces at the camera, then beaming smiles at one another.

Lilith stepped into Arnold's personal space bubble, angled her hips so that she was at a diagonal to the camera, rested one hand between his shoulder blades and the other on his chest. Her hair tickled Arnold's nose, and she smelled of roses and hairspray. Arnold tried to swallow but his mouth had gone dry.

Then off to the races. James was flush-faced and grinning as Ellie took his arm, while Arnold let Lilith walk in front of him toward his car, a cream-colored Honda Civic. He opened the passenger door for her, then looped around the car, slid into the driver's seat, and turned on the engine. Bon Jovi exhaled through the stereo, and Arnold quickly shut it off, blanketing the car in silence as he backed out of the driveway.

"How long are you planning to stay tonight?" Arnold asked. He drove with both hands on the wheel, eyes fastidiously latched onto the road.

"Not the whole time." Lilith was gazing out the window, her face awash with the streetlights. "Probably for at least a couple hours. And I don't have after party plans or anything, do you?"

"No. I was planning on heading out pretty early."

"Oh, that's okay, we can leave early."

"Okay." Silence, for a couple streetlights, painting the car in red light, green light, green light. "Lilith, why did you say yes?" Arnold was clenching his jaw.

"Well . . ." Lilith's eyes narrowed, and she clasped her fingers together. "Ellie should have said yes outright to James, and she didn't. This was the—albeit *ridiculous*—criteria Ellie set, so here we are." Calm silence. Red light, green light. "And I'm glad to go with you. You're one of my oldest friends. It'll be nice to spend prom together." Arnold didn't respond.

The entrance to their high school's parking lot saved Arnold from a long stretch of silence. He cruised through the rows, looking for open spots.

"I'll try to park closer. For your shoes," Arnold said. The dance was starting in about two minutes, and the parking lot was already bursting. He found a spot not too far away, but still a bit of a walk to the doors of the gymnasium, where the dance was being held. Lilith slid gracefully out of the car, and her three-inch, silver heels clicked against the parking lot as she rounded the driver's side and met Arnold. He held out his elbow and said, "Here, if you need to catch your balance."

Lilith looped her arm through his and rested her opposite hand on his bicep. "Thank you," she murmured.

The gymnasium was spastic in its decoration. Just inside the doors was a folding table draped in a cheap, white-plastic sheet, where Mr. Alvarez and Ms. Summer were selling and collecting tickets. Beyond that was a creamy-white balloon arch, and the decoration devolved from there. The bleachers had been collapsed and pressed against the side of the room. From the ceiling hung blue, white, and gold balloons and streamers, but the DJ lights were dominating the color scheme. The dancefloor pulsated with ear-damaging music and glittered with red, purple, and green flashing club lights.

"I can cover tickets," Lilith said, finally letting go of Arnold's arm to reach for her crossbody clutch, but Arnold reached into his pocket and pulled out two slightly crumpled tickets.

"I already got them."

"Oh." Lilith flushed and smiled at her shoes. They handed the tickets off to Ms. Summer, then they were sauntering through the arch, Lilith still on Arnold's arm. They joined the crowd of dancers, jumping up and down to "Gonna Make you Sweat (Everybody Dance Now)" by C+C Music Factory.

Lilith had let go of Arnold's arm, but as the songs switched and time wore on, she was inching closer to Arnold. Her hips swayed a little bit more, her smile grew a little bit wider. When the music slowed, and arms began looping around necks and hands gripped waists, Lilith reached for Arnold's collar. He took a forceful step backward and said, "I'll go get us some punch."

"Oh, yea, sure, thanks." Lilith grabbed her elbow with one hand and let her other arm dangle, then carefully extricated herself from the dancefloor, so she wouldn't be the only single dancer in a sea of couples.

The punch table was set off to the side, full of a half-depleted cherry-punch bowl, clear-plastic cups, nearly empty trays of blue-frosting cupcakes, and napkins. Arnold dipped a ladle into the punch bowl, just as Thomas Schroeder clapped Arnold on the shoulder and hollered, "Arnie! My man, how's it going?" The punch dribbled over Arnold's fingers, and Arnold tilted his head toward Thomas.

"Good, how about you?" Thomas' blonde hair was slicked back with sweat, his tie was loosened, and the top few buttons on his white dress shirt were undone. Arnold didn't know him too well, beyond having intermittent math classes together over the years.

"Pretty fine. Dude, is it true that you came with Lilith?"

Arnold's shoulders tensed, and he clutched his plastic punch cup tight enough to bend the sides inward. "Yea, so that James could take Ellie." He pointed out the couple on the dance floor, right after the slow song morphed into the opening of a rock song. Ellie and James were boogying down, wiggling their bums like a cat waiting to leap and flapping their arms like baby chickens.

"Okay, that makes more sense," Thomas laughed. "Ellie's a doll, looking out for Lilith like that. Lilith's pathetic. Good on you for at least giving her a pity date. Let her have one night. Sucks you couldn't take someone out for real though."

Arnold's brow creased and he clenched the cup tighter. More punch poured over his fingers. "Excuse me?"

Thomas held his hands up in an *I surrender* motion. "Sorry, man, thought I was preaching to the choir. I'm sure it's killing you that she's valedictorian. She totally doesn't deserve it." Thomas took the cup Arnold was pouring for Lilith out of Arnold's hand and downed what was left of it in one gulp. "I'm throwing an after party later tonight, you should come."

"I'll think on it," Arnold huffed. He craned his neck around Thomas to find Lilith, and there she was, twirling in small circles and bobbing her head in time to the beat. He marched toward her, grabbed the inside of her elbow with the tips of his fingers, and leaned close to her ear, once again embraced by the soft scent of roses and hairspray, and said, "I'm ready to call it a night."

Lilith frowned and scanned the gymnasium walls for a caged-in clock. It hadn't even been an hour yet. "Can't we stay a little longer?" she asked. Arnold clenched his jaw. "What's wrong, what happened?"

"Nothing."

"Let's talk outside." They hurried off the dancefloor—weaving through spastic, thrashing dancers and lip-locked, handsy couples—then out one of the gymnasium's side doors. They hovered on the concrete sidewalk. There was rustling in the bushes to their left, either an animal or a couple.

"Nothing happened," Arnold said, crossing his arms.

"You're lying to me."

Arnold sighed. "I took you to the dance, Ellie went with James, it's been a successful night. Let's call it here."

"Is that really the only reason you asked me to the dance? Because Ellie and James made you?" Lilith was shivering in her dress, arms crossed protectively in front of her stomach.

"Yes." Lilith's lower lip trembled, and she cleared her throat once. Twice. Arnold loosely grabbed Lilith's shoulders and said, "Look, Lilith, I'm not a school dance type of guy. You can still go have fun, have a friend drive you home or something."

"I only wanted a fun evening with *you,*" Lilith murmured. Her head was bowed, and Arnold couldn't see her eyes.

Arnold snarled and let go of Lilith's shoulders. "We hate each other! Why did you think this would be fun?"

"Would you just grow up, Arnold!" Lilith shrieked. She was hugging herself and trying to take deep breaths and, oh no, was she crying? Tears carved pristine tracks in her makeup, under-eye to jaw, rivulets that with time could carve a canyon. "And I *don't* hate you! In case that wasn't obvious tonight." Then she was turning away, disappearing back into the gymnasium, her shoulders scrunched up yet head held high.

6

CLEVELAND, OHIO DECEMBER 1992

The coffee shop was hazy, with sparse, navy-blue-shelled lamps hanging from the ceiling. It was a gloomy, stormy day, meaning the three walls consisting of floor-to-ceiling windows no longer illuminated the shop as brilliantly as they were designed to. Lilith was sitting at a circular, oakwood, two-person table in the corner, caged in by glass, cradling a steaming caramel macchiato, waiting. In between nervous sips, she brushed her curled hair back behind her ears with her fingers. Every time the door swished open and a new customer's shoes clicked against the gray linoleum floor, she jumped.

Arnold had asked her to meet him here—she glanced up at the ornamental wire clock hanging above the front door—fifteen minutes ago. He'd sent a message through James and Ellie. They were all back for winter break now, Arnold, James, and Lilith. James was practically living at the Hubbard household, inseparable from

Ellie, but in his spare moments, he could be found in his superhero bedroom, usually accompanied by Arnold.

Lilith didn't know what to expect from this meeting. Her chest ached dully, and her bright red, mock neck, long sleeve top was growing tighter by the minute. She hadn't seen Arnold since prom, except for in classes, when he pointedly ignored her, and at graduation, when he was curiously silent for the duration of her speech.

Maybe it had something to do with James and Ellie. Maybe he was finally apologizing. They both attended Ohio State now, and she was dreading and dreaming of a run-in with him. It was only a matter of time. Maybe he was here to sweep her off her feet, like slipping on a patch of black ice.

No. Lilith shook her head and ignored how her cheeks flushed. It was clear how Arnold felt about her. His *We hate each other*! had echoed through the folds of her brain since prom. She'd spent the majority of her secondary education pining after this guy, and to hear how he really felt about her—on what she'd hoped was their first date, no less—had sent her into a week-long wallow-fest. Ellie kept Lilith supplied with a steady stream of Reese's, Oreos, and romcom VHS rentals from the Blockbuster across town.

The bells hung on the coffee shop's front door dinged, and there was Arnold, in dark wash jeans and a light wash jean jacket with a black undershirt. His dark hair had grown out a couple inches since graduation, the last time Lilith had seen him. Arnold spotted Lilith at her corner table, and instead of joining the line to order, he hurried over. He slid into the empty seat, leaned back comfortably, then said, "I've been an idiot."

"Oh . . . kay?" Lilith replied. She swiped self-consciously at her upper lip with the side of her pointer finger, hoping there weren't remnants from her caramel macchiato.

"I judged you when we were kids, and never gave you a chance as we grew up, and I'm sorry for that." He watched Lilith through his lashes.

"Um." Lilith clutched her drink tighter. "What . . . prompted this? What changed?"

"I grew up?" Arnold offered.

"That's a shit answer."

"Yea, it is." Arnold dragged his fingers through his hair. He was wearing gold rings on three of them, and they reflected the few beams of light glittering down from the light fixture directly overhead. His hair tangled around one of his rings, and rather than fight against the metal, he yanked out the strands with a diminutive wince.

"I've seen you around campus," Arnold explained. "A few times, actually, and I don't know if you've seen me, but whenever I see you, I think about you for the rest of the day. The way that you smile when you're with your friends, and . . . And just how happy you look. You've been mentioned by mutual friends, and people respect you. You're known around campus for how smart and nice you are, and I just—" Arnold ran his hands through his hair again, this time his rings not tangling with his locks. "I've realized that I misjudged you."

Lilith's eyes were wide. She watched Arnold somewhat blankly, torn between dissolving into a pile of flattered mush and screaming in his face. All she did was whisper, "Oh," into her coffee before taking another sip.

"You don't have to say anything, if you don't want to," Arnold bleakly replied. He was sinking lower in his chair, bordering on slouching. The front of his jean jacket gaped open. "I just, after all this time, wanted to tell you the truth. I *don't* hate you. I think you're one of the most incredible people I've ever known."

Lilith flushed and her shoulders scrunched up. "Wow, Arnie, I—" She took a deep breath. "To be honest, I've wanted to hear you say that for years. I just don't know if I believe you. All you've given me are words." She let her head tilt to the side, and she set her nearly empty coffee on the table, then laid her hands flat against the wood.

Arnold perked up in his chair, one of his hands also resting on the table, his fingertips a couple inches away from Lilith's. "When we get back to campus, let me take you out."

"Like, a date?"

"Or friends! Whatever you're comfortable with." Arnold sighed and pressed his forehead into the palm of the hand that wasn't yearning for Lilith's.

"Let's start right now. See how things go." Lilith shrugged gracefully and pointed at the counter. "Get me a hot chocolate?"

"Yes. Of course." Then Arnold was out of his seat and scurrying into line. Lilith watched him, watched the way he fiddled with his rings. She teased her lower lip between her teeth. A small voice, a voice that was growing quieter by the second, was telling her that the past was the past. Arnold belonged there, as an unrequited schoolgirl crush. But an overwhelming voice was pterodactyl-screeching in joy. He'd finally seen her.

7

Columbus, Ohio, April 1993

"The long-sleeved top is better," Arnold was saying. He and Lilith were in Lilith's dorm, the bed littered with outfit options while Arnold reclined in the desk chair. They were due at a frat party Arnold's roommate, Roger, had invited them to in five minutes, yet they were still going in circles about what Lilith should wear.

"I like this one," Lilith said, propping her hands on her hips. She was wearing a zebra-striped tube top, her freckled shoulders bare.

"I don't like the message that sends," Arnold said, eyeing Lilith's shoulders not in desire but in scrutiny. "And you'll be cold."

"This is what I'm wearing," Lilith said with finality. "I like it." Arnold clenched his jaw and didn't say anything more. "Let's go."

They had been officially together for three months now. Their first coffee 'date' turned into two, into three, into Arnold asking Lilith to be his girlfriend the week before they went back to campus, and they'd been together since. Lilith, an English major, and Arnold, a Finance major, rarely crossed paths during the school day. The closest they got to a shared class was their Chemistry 101 course, same professor, different times. But they shared dining hall breakfasts of egg omelets and syrup-drenched overcooked pancakes, were going out to parties Friday and Saturday nights, and spent Sundays in their pajamas watching action movies. Lilith's stomach fluttered every time Arnold told her she was brilliant or beautiful, and Arnold couldn't help but brag about Lilith with every other breath.

They were walking hand in hand, Arnold's rings pressing into Lilith's fingers, across campus, toward the frat house. It was a warm spring evening, hinting at the summer to come. Lilith's boots clicked against the sidewalk concrete, and her free hand was wrapped around Arnold's arm.

The frat house was a couple stories tall, white, and with two cream pillars guarding the front doors, which were closed. The party was in the front yard, with at least a couple hundred people already writhing along to rock music with red, plastic cups in their hands. The yard was surrounded with a black-tarp fence, with one gap to allow invited guys and any girl in.

Once inside, Arnold spotted Roger right away. He was standing with a group of guys, sipping on a beer. Arnold and Lilith joined the circle.

"Arnie!" Roger bellowed, cuing Lilith in on his already inebriated state. "Drinks?" Roger grabbed a couple unopened beers from a red-and-white cooler behind him and handed them to Arnold and Lilith. Arnold popped his open with his keys and drank a quarter of it in one long swig. Lilith held hers, unopened, as a prop.

"Arnie, was it?" one of the other guys, probably the only sober guy of the group, standing there said. "You're the chemistry guy."

"Oh," Arnold's eyes widened slightly, and he pasted on a toothy grin. "Yup, that's me." He took another quarter-bottle swig.

"Would you be able to tutor me? Before the next exam, I mean."

"No school!" Roger interjected, staring daggers, and holding his beer out in front of him in a vaguely hostile gesture. He karate-chopped the air with his free hand and reiterated, "No school."

"I could pay, no problem," the guy continued.

"I'll let you know," Arnold said.

Lilith was staring at Arnold with a raised eyebrow. She distinctly remembered Arnold gloomy for an entire day after he got his 72 back on the last exam. Arnold wouldn't look at her. Quarter-bottle swig. Reaching for Lilith's unopened beer. She gave it to him.

The next couple hours passed with uneventful small-talk and bodies bobbing up and down to music blaring too loud to discern intelligible lyrics. Arnold was off talking to someone, both laughing uncontrollably, both five beers in. Lilith, still sober, and Roger, who stopped drinking when Arnold and Lilith arrived, were sitting in the grass, leaning against the external wall of the frat house, talking shit about their respective high schools. The party burbled around them, vibrating with beat drops and quaking with intoxication, but they'd carved out a bubble to sit, watch, observe.

"Tell me, was Arnie a jock?" Roger asked, pointing at Arnold across the yard. "I can kind of see it, but also can't."

"Oh, not at all!" Lilith cackled. It was close to midnight, the air now frigid and Lilith regrettably shivering and rubbing her arms. "Think momma's boy, obsessed with school, and then add in a pinch of douchebag."

"Ha! Now that is more believable. Was he valedictorian or something?"

"Not quite. I beat him out for that title."

Roger's jaw dropped slightly, then he leaned his head back against the wall. "I bet the chem grades must be killing you, then."

Lilith tilted her head to the side. "What do you mean?"

Roger sat up straight and held his hands aloft in the air. "Oh, sorry, Arnie told me about your C- and his A+." He pressed his hand across his mouth and whisper-yelled, "Was that secret boyfriend stuff he wasn't supposed to tell me?"

Lilith frowned. "Not secret stuff. Just lies. Last I checked, the A+ was mine."

"Oh."

"Huh."

Roger and Lilith leaned back against the wall at the same time, their heads angled backward, so that their noses were tilted toward the light-polluted night's sky.

"Arnie told me last night that he wants to break up with you before this summer," Roger admitted. He didn't look at Lilith but kept staring upwards. "You should beat him to it."

Lilith sighed deeply, tears beading on her lower lashes and her chest aching. "I will." She let her gaze fall from the sky to Arnold, to him quarter-chugging another beer. "Once he sobers up."

"I guess this is goodbye, then," Roger said. "Between us."

"I guess so." They shook hands, her dry palm against his clammy fingers.

"Take care of him," Lilith whispered, as Roger crouched, stood, wiped clumps of grass from his pants, and walked away.

8

New York City, March 2022

"I broke up with him the next morning," Lilith said. Alice was holding her hand, the two women sitting side by side with their foreheads pressed together. "He was angry that *I* broke up with *him*. I was in pain, and he cared more about getting the upper hand than about me."

"I'm sorry, Aunt Lilith," Alice whispered. Her eyes were droopy, and she'd yawned through the last twenty minutes of Aunt Lilith's story. Her chest ached, just as Lilith's had on that night, just as it had been aching over her own heartbreak.

"Oh, don't be sorry! I learned so much during those three months with him. My First Great Heartbreak isn't about losing him, but about losing me." Lilith brushed Alice's hair behind her ear. "Arnold cared so much about what other people thought, and I didn't. I started placing higher value in what Arnold thought, but his head was full of the opinions of others. I poured so much of myself into that relationship, time and effort spent on a guy that cared for me a fraction of the amount I cared for him.

"He could be kind and devoted and loyal, but he could also lie and pretend. In the ensuing months, I picked apart what I wanted in a partner, and what I never wanted again. I also realized how infantile our relationship was. Dating in college doesn't make a romantic relationship one between adults. I should have left him in my high school past, and I didn't. I should have listened to the little voice in my head telling me the relationship wasn't healthy for me."

Alice nodded, then yawned. She was verging into the realm of no longer comprehending what Lilith was telling her. "Thank you for sharing."

"Of course, my sweet."

"And. It was nice to hear about my parents. They don't talk about being in high school."

Lilith hummed and stood, making her way toward the door. "I hope that one day, my sister will tell you the whole truth of her love story with your dad, because it was not without its difficulties. For now, though, get some sleep. This will be a busy week for you. Tomorrow morning Robin can go with you to your dorm to get your things."

"Okay." Alice rubbed at her burning eyes. "Thank you."

"Goodnight, dear. Oh, and take that kitchen knife back with you!"

Lilith let the door swing closed behind her, and Alice rifled through the dresser to find the clothes Lilith offered earlier. She found an oversized Motley Crüe T-shirt and flannel drawstring pants. Alice was too numb to sort through her feelings, yearning to drown out every emotion except exhaustion. She changed into the borrowed clothes, climbed into the bed, burrowed into fresh sheets that smelled of rosemary, and sank into the goose down pillows.

Yet despite her heavy exhaustion, Alice remembered that day, the day she met Rylan in the coffee shop.

Alice was walking with her roommate, Devi Khatri, on a crisp autumn morning, their boots clicking against cracked sidewalks, their hair drawn up in messy buns, and arms linked together, their heads nearly pressed together, Alice's strawberry blonde hair and Devi's warm brown hair contrasting and complimenting. A firetruck and police car were approaching on the street to their right, sirens squealing. As it passed, they scrunched up their shoulders.

"I hate it here," Devi whispered. Devi was from a tiny, rural Wisconsin town, a place devoid of disaster where everybody knew everybody and there were more police escorts for out-of-town football games than there were need for police cars. New York City was . . . an adjustment to say the least.

Alice just pressed her lips together in a soft smile. She was from Seattle, and all things considered, Seattle to New York City wasn't too great a leap. New York City was growing on her by the day.

Their destination was three minutes' walk down the sidewalk, to a quaint coffee shop continuously overrun with Columbia and Barnard students. It was two stories. The first had a long, cherrywood counter from which a perpetual ten-to-fifteen-person-long line originated. A series of circular, black-metal tables with four chairs apiece littered the rest of the space. On the walls hung black-and-white photographs in thick gray frames. A spiral staircase in the back corner led to the second floor, where the metal table and monochrome photography motif continued, but there was also a fireplace with three black-leather loveseats around it and gray-cushioned booths situated against the walls beneath tall windows with thick panes. Alice thought the place was too masculine and needed a pop of color, but Devi disagreed.

Alice and Devi stood in the monstrous line and ordered matching cappuccinos, then lucked out and snagged an upstairs booth with a view out onto the bustling street below. They pulled sticker-covered computers and spiral notebooks from their backpacks and started bickering over the correct way to solve for velocity in problem number six of their physics homework. This was their Saturday morning tradition, ever since they moved in a little over a month ago. Cappuccinos, homework, and, eventually, goofing off. But they weren't quite there yet that morning.

"Devi?"

Alice and Devi pulled themselves out of their final physics homework problem—finding the velocity of a squirrel jumping out of a tree—to see a tall, lean, blue-sweater-vest-wearing, brunet with his arms crossed over his chest. "Charlie?" Devi replied, shaking her head and laughing. She launched herself out of the booth and wrapped Charlie in a big hug. Charlie's eyes widened, and his reciprocation of the hug was an awkward pat on Devi's shoulder. After five more uncomfortable seconds, Devi pulled away and turned back to look at Alice. "Alice, this is Charlie, one of my friends from back home!" Her head whipped back around, her messy bun threatening to unravel, and said, "What are you doing here?"

"I'm visiting one of my buddies that goes to Columbia." Charlie pointed over his shoulder with his thumb to a booth across the room of three other guys. "I saw you and thought I'd come over and say hi. You're welcome to join us, if you'd like."

Devi clasped her hands together and gave puppy dog eyes to Alice. "Physics homework can wait?" Devi pleaded.

Alice shook her head and giggled, "It unfortunately can't." Devi wilted, her head drooping, her crimson red sweater slipping awkwardly off her shoulder, her arms dangling lifelessly toward the ground. "But we'll be over once we finish up," Alice conceded.

"Sounds great," Charlie said, then he hurried back to his booth.

"What's his story?" Alice asked as Devi slid into her seat.

"Charlie and I have known one another since preschool, and we were good friends in middle school." Devi sighed and began unpinning her hair, so that it hung in a straight sheet past her shoulder blades. "Then I got the *biggest* crush on him in high school and didn't know how to talk to him anymore."

"So is today friend or boyfriend motivated?"

"Friend! I swear friend!" Devi shook her hands spastically in the air. "But also boyfriend if, you know, he initiates something. *I'm* not going to. But if he does, why not?"

"Ohhh-kaaaay," Alice sang. They hurried through the last velocity problem—getting an answer of the squirrel was traveling 352.6 meters per second, which did not sound right, but it was what they were going with—packed up their things, and approached Charlie's booth.

"Guys, this is Devi," Charlie said, scooting over to make room for Devi to sit on the edge of the bench seat next to him. "And this is her friend . . ."

"I'm Alice," Alice supplied, sitting on the edge of the seat opposite Devi, next to one of the strange guys. "We're roommates at Barnard."

"We're all roommates at Columbia," one of the guys said. He was wearing a gray sweater that said, "Got Milk?" in white letters across the chest. "Except for Charlie, he's my buddy from camp." He was sitting on the other side of Charlie and clapped him on the back with a cupped palm. "I'm Sullivan."

"Darius." The guy sitting closest to the wall on Alice's side. He was reading a book, the cover a deep brown but the title obscured. He didn't look up from his page.

"Rylan." The towhead blond sitting directly beside Alice. He gave Alice a small wave, raising his left hand with his pinkie and third finger folded over.

"Where are you all from?" Alice asked, but she was promptly ignored. Devi, Charlie, and Sullivan were already engrossed in an anecdote about meeting at camp, Devi making googly eyes at Charlie, and Darius refusing to look up from his book.

"I'm from Green Bay, Wisconsin," Rylan said. He shifted in the booth, so his torso was diagonally facing Alice and his back was to Darius. "What about you?"

"Seattle."

"Long way away from home for you, then!"

"I prefer it that way, to be honest." Alice brushed a strand of hair that had escaped her bun behind her ear. "I get a chance to be on my own. It's nice to be away."

"Ah, I see, running wild now that you're out of the house?"

Alice held up her hand, palm up. "No! Not like that," she amended. "More like, it's nice being able to go out and do whatever I want, whenever I want. Green Bay is a fair bit away, too, what brought you out here?"

"My parents met at Columbia," Rylan sighed, "so I'm here chasing a fairytale romance." He batted his eyelashes until Alice giggled. "Naw, Columbia's a great school, I'm proud to be second-gen. New York is such a cool city, too."

"It is! I do get intimidated, though. It's so big, I'm worried I'll get lost!" Alice laughed and brushed her hair behind her ears again. "That also might just be my mom's voice, though. Ever since I committed to Barnard, she was on me about being aware of my surroundings, not straying too far from campus, safety in numbers."

"I could take you out, sometime, if you'd like."

"Take . . . me out? Alice stuttered, her stomach doing backflips. She'd never been asked out before. "Like a date?"

"Er, uh," Rylan replied, "if you wanted it to be, yea." He was flushed, his features a bit pinched in anticipation.

"Um, okay."

"Okay."

"Can I get your number?" As Alice created a new contact for herself in his phone, he asked, "Are you free next Friday?"

"Yes."

"I'll text you details, then."

"Okay."

Rylan and Alice spent the following twenty minutes listening intently to Charlie's camp story about how he and Sullivan had gotten lost in the woods after two girls promised to meet them there. They ignored Devi's googly eyes. They inched closer and closer to one another, until their sides were pressed together.

The familiar ache in Alice's chest deepened, the pain radiating outward to caress her shoulders. Part of her regretted that day. If she and Devi had just stayed at their dorm, picked a different coffee shop, Alice wouldn't feel splintered in two, a ravine carved through her chest.

Alice took a deep breath, inhaling the fragrant vanilla, lavender, and balsam air into her lungs and holding it there, then expelling it with a huff. Her hair splayed out onto the pillowcase like vines sprawled across a brick building. Out in the hall, the flowers breathed.

Settle In

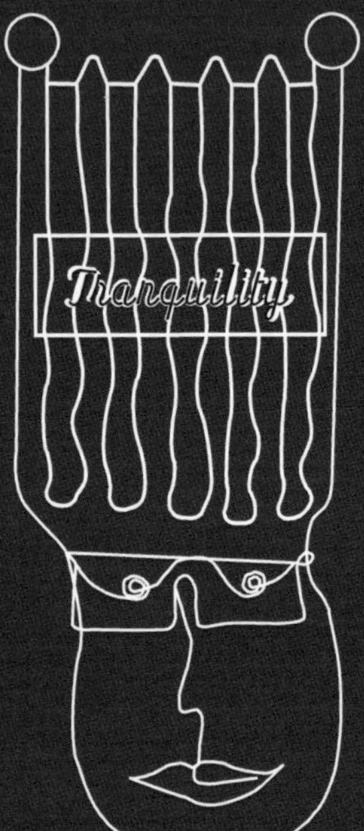

2

9

New York City, March 2022

"Good morning!" Robin chirped. He was standing in front of the reception desk wearing dark wash jeans, gray tennis shoes, and a sky-blue, long-sleeved button-down. Behind him, the cluttered butterfly-walled paintings flapped greetings in Alice's peripheral vision. "Ready?"

"Yes," Alice yawned. She was wearing her pink peacoat, just the kitchen knife in her pocket this time. She'd left Lilith's letter on the nightstand.

"I thought we'd walk there. Give our legs a stretch."

"Sure."

They departed Tranquility and joined the crowd of New Yorkers making their way around Manhattan on a bustling Saturday morning. The vanilla, lavender, and Christmas tree scent of Tranquility gave way to petrichor with an undertone of sewage.

"Did you settle in alright?" Robin asked. He walked with his hands tucked in his jean pockets and hummed quietly, the same tune that Lilith sang last night. Every twenty paces or so, Robin pushed his glasses back up his nose.

"Yes, Aunt Lilith is so kind." Alice tucked her hands into the pocket of her peacoat to mirror Robin. The knife handle bounced against her knuckles. "Do you live at Tranquility?"

"Me? No," Robin chuckled, "I don't need to anymore. I have an apartment a few blocks over. Lilith lives at Tranquility, though. So does Vincent, one of the bartenders, and Carmela and Enid, a couple of the singers. Have you met them yet?"

"Briefly." Alice stared down at her kitten-heeled black boots and bit her lip. "I guess Aunt Lilith told everyone why I'm here, then," she whispered.

"Oh, no!" Robin stopped walking and grabbed Alice by the shoulders, his strong fingers creating individual divots in the fabric of her peacoat. The crowd parted around them, the occasional elbow or shoulder jostling their backs. "Lilith told me that you were her niece, and that you might visit during your spring break. That's it. And that's more than she told the others. She doesn't betray people like that. We get to dictate who knows our story here." Robin let go of Alice and continued walking, hands back in his pockets.

"Although," Robin continued, "Now that you're here, we've assumed that you'd had your heart broken. Tranquility is a place that can't be found unless your heart has been broken before."

Alice nodded. She watched Robin in her peripheral vision, noting his graying temples, the laugh lines beneath his eyes. "How long have you known Lilith?"

"Years," Robin answered quickly. He tapped the side of his bent index finger against his chin as he thought.

"Around thirteen years, give or take a couple. Time blurs together after so many years spent similarly. But I'll tell you all about how I met Lilith later, don't you worry. Something you should know is that Lilith will try and make your stay here overly dramatic and life changing. You are here to spend a week wallowing in your feelings if you feel the need, living under a roof and eating food you don't have to pay for, and getting to know a group of people that will, hopefully, make you feel less alone."

"Last night, Aunt Lilith made it sound like after this week I'd be a different person or something," Alice said.

"Not at all. Lilith likes to hand out life lessons like free samples, even though she's not very good at it in the short-term." Alice conjured a mental image of her aunt handing out food samples at Costco and couldn't help but giggle.

They arrived at Alice's dorm building, a stately brown-brick edifice rife with windows, and Alice hurried up to her room to pack a bag, taking the stairs two at a time. Robin waited for her outside the building, insisting that Alice take her time and make sure to grab everything she needed.

Alice unlocked her dorm with her copper-toned key and as the door swung open, it wafted stale air. Devi had already cleared out for the break. Her side of the dorm was curiously neat, with the grey paisley duvet tucked neatly around her mattress and her closet doors actually able to shut completely, now that she'd filled an entire suitcase with clothes. Alice's side of the dorm was unkempt. Her desk was strewn with paper handouts from professors, and the three knit blankets on her bed were askew. On the windowsill were their plant babies: Candy the Cactus and Alfred Aloe. Their soil was still damp from when Alice watered before leaving for Tranquility.

Alice pulled her carry-on luggage out from beneath her lofted bed with its lilac purple casing, a graduation gift from her grandparents. She stuffed inside a couple pairs of jeans, leggings, sweaters, blouses, underwear, sports bras, the black-lace lingerie she bought herself to feel like an adult but had never worn before, a bodycon dress, fuzzy socks, a pair of white tennis shoes wrapped in a plastic Target bag, a zippered pouch of eyeshadow, eyeliner, mascara, and lipstick, and her royal-blue retainer. She had to sit on the luggage to get it to zipper closed.

Next, Alice dumped the contents of her backpack—astrology and calculus II textbooks, three pads of sticky notes, and a calendar—onto her disheveled bed. Into her backpack went the printed instructions for her English lit essay due a couple days after break, her toothbrush, toothpaste, and hairbrush, paperback copies of *Moby-Dick* and *Frankenstein*, and her computer, plus chargers for her phone and computer.

Alice rifled through the paper handouts on her desk to ensure she didn't miss anything she needed, and she unwittingly picked up the stack of love letters from Rylan. She stilled and stared at the crinkled envelopes. Ever since their breakup, she'd been rereading them and binge-reading their text messages, over and over. The last time he texted her, "I love you." The apologies on nights he blew off their plans. Countless puppy-eye emojis. He'd promised that he'd send her one last letter, a farewell love letter, after they'd broken up, but Alice had been kept waiting for nearly a month now.

Alice stuffed the letters into her backpack. After she scanned her dorm room one last time, she pulled the letters back out of the bag. There were three of them, all from winter break with matching envelopes and rose-bedecked notecards. Alice perched on the end of her bed and slid the notecard out of the first letter. She brushed her finger against the embossed petals of a blush-pink rose and flipped the letter open. It was the most romantic letter of the three.

"My dear Alice," the card read in Rylan's squat handwriting, *"How's it going? I miss you. I miss holding you in my arms. I miss—"* Alice's eyes skipped down to the end of the letter. *"Only four weeks until I can kiss you again. Affectionately yours, Rylan."* Two tears raced down Alice's face, one slipping across her nose and the other dripping past her mouth to her chin. She scrubbed her cheeks with her palms and shoved the letter back into its envelope with such force that the envelope ripped open.

She left the three letters on her desk. Made sure the kitchen knife was resting beside the letters. Locked her dorm behind her.

In the time between then and Alice's return, a single red rose would bloom from the love letters, sprouting from their recycled paper. The rose would wilt and die. Alice would puzzle over the puddle of pollen and the single, vibrant petal perched atop the love letters before sweeping all of it directly into the trash—Rylan's squat handwriting and all.

IO

New York City, March 2022

Alice was sitting at the bar in Tranquility. She'd had a successful late morning and early afternoon of unpacking, with a good hour snack break, and was now watching Vincent and Mateo wipe down the counter and rearrange bottles as they prepared for the evening.

Alice was scrolling through her phone. Devi had texted her, letting her know that she and her family landed in Madrid and that though she wouldn't be able to stay in contact, she hoped Alice had a great break. There were two missed calls from her mom, and one voicemail. "Lilith let me know that you're there safe and sound," her mother's pithy voice crackled over the speakers, "I hope you have a great week. We'll miss you."

Alice hadn't seen Lilith since the previous evening, aside from thirty minutes ago when Lilith dashed through the dining room carrying at least ten feather boas, leaving a trail of multicolored feathers in her wake.

"So," Vincent said, drawing Alice's attention to him. He had his hands resting on the counter, his cleaning rag pinned beneath his right palm. "Would you like to hear my Great Heartbreak?" His controlled smile was teeming with barely restrained glee.

"Sure," Alice replied, tucking her phone into the back pocket of her jeans, leaning forward, and resting her elbows on the counter.

"Vince, can you go get more glasses?" Mateo asked from a couple paces away.

Vincent pinched his lips and his shoulders hunched inward, but he quickly said, "Sure thing!" to Mateo and, "be right back," to Alice. At Vincent's retreating footsteps, Mateo slid down the bar, wiping down a greasy spot Vincent missed.

"Once he gets the glasses put under the counter, he can sit down and talk to you," Mateo promised. He was a middle-aged gentleman, with a thick head of brown hair, tan skin, and a gray-speckled goatee. "How have you been enjoying Tranquility so far?"

"It's been a bit intense," Alice confessed. She sat on her hands and leaned back in her chair. "But I think staying here will be good for me."

"I know it was for me. I lived here about five years ago, helped me get back on my feet."

"After your Great Heartbreak?"

Mateo sighed, then chuckled to himself. "Yea, that would be Lilith's term for it. We've all been where you are, beaten down and hurting, and then we found this place, or Lilith found us, and we've all gone through the storytelling ordeal. I empathize with you." Mateo tossed his cleaning rag into the sink along the back counter. "The last person to go through this was Vincent. He's overexcited to get a chance to tell his story for the first time."

Alice nodded and pulled her numbing fingers out from beneath her thighs, crossing her hands in her lap. "How long have you been here?"

"Nearly as long as Lilith. She bought the place in . . ." Mateo squinted one of his eyes closed as he thought it through. "2000? 2001? Something like that. And then we met at a concert a couple years later, she did her Lilith intuition thing, and I've worked here ever since." Mateo's eyes softened, and his shoulders relaxed. "I met my husband here, while bartending one night, and our daughter is six now. It's funny how life works out sometimes."

Vincent returned with the glasses, two stacked, plastic, webbed crates in his arms. He set them gingerly on the counter, then one-by-one slid them onto shelves beneath it.

"Well, before you start talking, Vince, might as well say my piece," Mateo said. He looked Alice directly in the eyes. "Over twenty years ago, my then-boyfriend cheated on me with my sister. When I found out, I was just about to ask him to move in with me. My sister got pregnant. My ex thought it was his kid, and it was not. Then he came back to me, groveling and apologizing. At the time, I still thought he was the love of my life, but I knew I had to turn him down, so I did. And now I'm here, happier than I could have fathomed in that moment."

"How'd you know you had to turn him down?" Alice asked quietly. She picked at a hangnail on her thumb. "How were you able to?"

"I couldn't see myself having children with him anymore." Mateo scratched his goatee with the pads of his fingers. "I'd always wanted children, and even though I could rationalize all the ways we as a couple could still work, I could no longer see him as a father to my future children. I would have let him walk all over me, but the thought of him betraying our future kid was enough for me to stand up for what was right. Hardest damn thing I've ever had to do, stare the man I loved with all my heart in his blue eyes and say, 'I never want to see you again.'"

Mateo held out his hand, palm up, across the bar and waited for Alice to take it. He pinched her fingers between his and said, "Find one thing outside yourself to stand up for. I found it's easier to respect others than it is to respect yourself." Alice squeezed Mateo's hand back.

Edith, Alice thought, staring at she and Mateo's hands, remembering.

It was a Wednesday during winter break. Alice had texted Rylan six hours ago, and still no response. Rylan wasn't working. He had no obligations besides spending time with family and friends. And Alice didn't understand why that meant it took him over six hours to reply.

"Good morning! Hope you have a good day. What time are you available to call later?" her text had read, sent at 8 a.m. her time, 10 a.m. his, as soon as she woke up. She'd been waiting by the phone since, sitting on the couch in the living room watching Hallmark movies with her dad.

"Allie, mom and I want to play Clue." Edith, Alice's little sister, was standing by the side of the couch. Her short hair—dark like their father's—was fanned out behind her head like peacock feathers, and there were sleep crusties around her eyes. She was still wearing her pajamas, pink and purple polka dot cotton pants and one of their dad's college debate team T-shirts. "We need you or else we can't play."

"Sure," Alice said, disentangling herself from the blanket she'd been ever-so-slowly melding with. It wasn't like she had anything else to do.

The two girls thundered down the creaky basement stairs to find the board game, and as Edith's bare feet pitter-pattered against the dusty, concrete floor, Alice's phone buzzed. "Hey! I can talk right now if you're free," a new text from Rylan read.

"Actually, can we play in like, an hour?" Alice asked. She was standing in the middle of the flight of stairs, phone clutched in both hands, staring down at her sister as Edith held a ripped-but-duct-taped-back-together Clue.

Edith frowned. "Mom's starting dinner in an hour."

"We can play after dinner, then."

"I guess."

Alice hurried up the stairs, to her bedroom, Face-Timing Rylan as she walked. He picked up on the fifth ring. "Hey, babe, how are you?" he asked. He was sitting on a couch in his living room, TV chatter in the background.

"I'm good, not much has happened today, what about you?" Alice replied as she settled into her oversized, pink-plush desk chair.

"Crazy morning! Bo and I drove out to visit his grandparents that live on a farm, and we spent the day riding horses, it was great! Now we're back at my house, and in fifteen minutes or so, we're going to go out to dinner with my parents."

"That's cool!" Alice's thoughts sagged. Rylan was spending time with his friend. He'd had a fun morning. She'd spent her time pining after him and waiting around. She was pathetic. She needed to be more understanding. But now, the "fifteen minutes" rang between her ears. "Where are you going for dinner?"

"Not sure, that's what's being decided right now. I should probably go join, they're all in the kitchen."

"Oh." Alice's brow furrowed. "Will I get to talk to you tonight?"

"Probably not," Rylan sighed. "I'm just really busy right now. I was thinking we could start talking in the mornings? Like, before 9am. Done talking by 9am? I'd have more time then."

"Oh. That's 7 a.m. my time." Alice was a mid-morning person. Waking up any time before 7 a.m. was a struggle, and sleeping in past 9 a.m. was impossible, unless her sleep schedule had been majorly disturbed. And now Rylan wanted to be *done* talking by 7 a.m.?

"Crap, I'd forgotten about that." Rylan dragged a hand down his face.

"No, no, it's okay. That'll work for me," Alice said. She smiled brightly at the camera. She could wake up early, talk to Rylan, then go back to sleep for an hour or so. Totally manageable.

"Are you sure? I know that's really early for you."

"I just want to be able to talk to you."

Rylan made kissy lips at the camera. "You're the best. I appreciate you."

Alice made the kissy lips back. "I miss you." She waited for Rylan to say it back, but as the seconds passed, he merely frowned, a crease forming between his eyebrows. "What's wrong?"

"Over the past few days, I've realized that I don't really miss things," he admitted. "I'm really adaptable to my surroundings."

"Oh."

"But that doesn't mean I don't care about you!" Rylan quickly amended. "Just because I don't miss you doesn't mean you're not important in my life." He stuck out his bottom lip and widened his eyes.

Alice's lips were pinched. "Okay," she said.

Someone offscreen called Rylan's name and Rylan sighed. "I've got to go. I'll talk to you tomorrow morning?"

"Yea, tomorrow morning."

Rylan made his kissy lips again, then hung up. Alice listened to the monotone beeping of her phone, then reread she and Rylan's text messages until her mom called her for dinner.

There Alice sat at the bar in Tranquility, her hand still gingerly held by Mateo's, thinking of Edith, thinking, "If Rylan and I stayed together, what example would that set for Edith? How many times had I ignored Edith for Rylan?"

Mateo squeezed Alice's hand one last time, then said, "The floor is yours, Vince." With that, Mateo clapped Vincent on the shoulder and headed through the black swinging doors to the kitchen.

Vincent checked his watch, nodded to himself, then motioned for Alice to join him on one of the red-velvet couches around the perimeter of the room, that blurred into the shadows. "That's pretty much word for word what he told me when I first got here," Vincent said as they walked, shaking his head. "I wonder how many times he's told people what he's been through, and if it's always been that succinct."

"You could ask him?" Alice suggested.

"Nah, let it be a mystery." They sat on a couch at an angle, twisted sideways to face one another. "Okay. Without further ado, this is the tale of my Great Heartbreak."

II

La Crosse, Wisconsin, September 2018

Vincent Hanson and Li Huang were walking side by side through the friendship garden, near the Mississippi riverfront in downtown La Crosse. Vincent was sweating. The nape of his neck was tacky with sweat, making his blond curls matte against his flesh. He tried to subtly wipe his clammy palms on his jeans as Li snapped photographs of blooming, purple pansies with her iPhone.

"Smile!" Li said, holding up her phone in its glittery, lime-green case and flipping the camera around to take a selfie. Vincent scooted closer and had enough time to give a floppy half-grin when Li took the photo. "Cute," she said, without even looking at it.

Vincent and Li were both juniors at the University of Wisconsin-La Crosse. He was studying Finance and French, and she Psychology and Political Science, both with law school dreams. They'd met in their British Literature class their freshman year, back when Vincent had shaved all his hair off on a dare from his roommate and Li was still getting accustomed to living in the Midwest after spending her entire life in the Pacific Northwest. Li plopped down in a seat behind Vincent, and as the semester passed, she noted the steady re-growth of his bouncy, blond curls.

She started talking to him. From "Do you have a pencil?" to, "What are you writing your essay about?" until finally, "Would you like to study for the final together?" Vincent had spent the semester ignoring the dimples in her cheeks when she smiled, ensuring he always had an extra-sharp pencil for her to borrow, and painting his fingernails a consistent royal purple after she said it was her favorite color. He nodded along with any little scrap of information she told him, whether it was about growing up in Seattle or what book she was reading that week. When she'd asked him to study together, he spent five hours reviewing their assigned readings prior to meeting up with her, so that he would be prepared to help with whatever she needed.

They studied together at the library, each scooting first their textbooks, then their chairs, closer together as the afternoon progressed. The semester concluded with sparkling A's for each of them. They exchanged phone numbers, but had too large a dose of fear to call one another. So the next semester passed, then the next, and the next, until now, their junior years, when a mutual friend reunited them at a concert.

"Vince!" Li had cheered, smiling at Vincent as he joined her and the friend group in line. They were standing outside the La Crosse Center, waiting in a queue that led from outside through the front doors. Li was wearing bellbottom jeans and a tight-fitting, cropped, orange-sorbet-colored, long-sleeve that shimmered with glitter.

"Hi, Li," Vincent replied, suddenly breathless.

After the concert—an evening of not-so-subtle glances—Li called Vincent one afternoon and said, point-blank. "I think you should hang out with me on Friday night."

"Okay," Vincent replied.

And now here they were, walking through the friendship garden, Vincent's insides broiling as he internally debated whether or not this was a date. *She used the words, 'hang out,'* he internally reasoned, *but we're also spending time together one-on-one looking at flowers and art installations.* Li gave him no further indication with her fluttery, flushed smiles. She wore distressed jeans and a purple blouse, not unusual from her regular attire, also not indicative of a date or not.

They were nearing the end of the concrete path and winding their way closer to the riverfront. The sun was setting, marbling the sky with pinks and yellows. Vincent subtly glanced at his watch. It wasn't even eight yet!

"I think we should still hang out," Li said. She was watching the river, then pointed at an empty bench a couple hundred feet away. "We can sit there?"

"Yea, sounds good," Vincent managed to reply.

They sat down, Vincent to the left, Li on the right, a solid foot of space between them. Vincent leaned back against the bench and fought to urge to put his arm around her.

"My mom sent me a care package last week that had fresh cookies in it," Li said. She shook her head, sleek black hair trembling as she did so. "I have no idea how she did it!" Vincent could feel the bench vibrate against his back as Li talked, the metal rumbling from Li's vocal cords.

"My mom once tried to send me a pie over thanksgiving. It did not go well," Vincent chuckled.

And then ensued two hours of talking, sharing stories from their childhoods, comparing professors and classes, asking mundane get-to-know you questions like, "Do you have siblings?" and, "What's your favorite animal?" The sunset quickly gave way to twilight, and the streetlights around them buoyed their bench in a sea of calm darkness.

At around ten, the foot of space between them had shrunk to a half-foot. Li took a deep breath and said, "I like you, Vince. Do you like me?"

"Yes!" Vincent blurted. He flushed and cleared his throat. "Yes, I like you. Romantically. I'm attracted to you."

Li smiled, demurely at first, trying to smother her excitement, but within a minute she was widely grinning, enough so that Vincent could see her molars.

And their conversation continued, except this time about difficult topics, the deep conversations, about dating history and sex, religion and core values, politics and beliefs, ambitions and dreams. By the end of their evening, when their eyelids were droopy, when Vincent's watch read midnight, their six inches of space had shrunk to nothing, and Vincent's arm was around Li's shoulders.

12

La Crosse, Wisconsin, September 2018

Vincent asked Li if she wanted to go out on a real date. She said yes with another molar-baring grin. They had a whirlwind week of movie nights and dinner dates, flirting and texting. They weren't official. Yet.

They were at a pizza place, sitting in the back corner at a two-person table. The lights were dimmed, and the walls were painted with murals of roses and psychedelic skulls. Li sat with her back against a painting of an open-mouthed skull with a blossomed rosebud between its teeth. Her hair was drawn up in an elegant, slightly tousled bun, and she wore ripped jeans, a black tank top, and a candy-apple-red jacket with ballet flats in a matching color. Vincent sat across from her in khakis, a navy-blue, short sleeve button-down, and loafers. His palms were sweating.

Vincent was going to ask Li to be his girlfriend. Tonight.

If she said yes, Vincent was going to kiss Li for the first time. Tonight.

They had ordered a large vegetable pizza to split and were waiting for the waiter to bring it out from the kitchen. Vincent was guzzling water, taking a sip every time his mouth was dry, and his mouth was continually dry. Desert sand gritty dry, nearly. He'd bypassed the straw, leaving it in its paper packaging. He instead widened his mouth along the glass rim as much as he could without spilling water down the sides of his face. Li had noticed the water consumption, both the amount and method, but didn't say anything.

Conversation had drifted to that of law school, yet another ambition they shared. "I want to study international law," Vincent was saying. "My ultimate dream is to work at a law firm in France."

"I've heard great things about the study abroad program!" Li replied.

"Me too!" Sip of water. "But not just study abroad. Like, permanently."

Li shifted in her seat and laced her fingers together, then pressed the side of her crossed pointer finger to her lips. "Permanently?"

"I want to settle down in France," Vincent clarified. He bit his lip. "Or maybe not France, per se," he amended, "but somewhere in Europe. Do you want to live in Europe?"

Li sat there, hands still pressed to her lips, and knew instantly that she had no desire to travel to Europe, let alone *live* in Europe. Vincent could read it in her face. "Um, maybe," she whispered. They each stared at the table. Vincent's mouth had gone dry, but for a different reason than nerves.

The waiter brought their pizza within the next two minutes, and they ate in silence. They each ate about a quarter of the pizza, far less than they normally were able to. When the waiter came back, Li asked for two to-go boxes. Vincent paid. Li offered to split the bill, but Vincent said he could cover it. They'd been taking turns paying for dinner all week and it was his turn.

They sat on a bench outside the restaurant, their respective to-go boxes in their laps, the six-inches between them imposed once more.

"I don't want to live in Europe," Li finally said.

"I know," Vincent whispered.

Li turned to look at him. A couple strands of hair had fallen out of her bun to frame her face, which glowed in the red light from the restaurant sign. "Of all the things I could compromise on in a relationship, this is one thing I can't. Where we'd live in the future. And I can't date you if I don't see a future with you. I wish I was that type of person, but I'm just not."

"I know," Vincent nodded, "I understand." He clutched his to-go box tighter and the Styrofoam crinkled beneath his fingers.

"I think you're an amazing person," Li said, her face scrunching up with an onslaught of tears, "and thank you for this week. It's been wonderful. I'm grateful for the time I got to spend getting to know you."

"You, too, Li."

Li took a couple deep breaths to stave off her tears. Vincent walked her back to her apartment building, hand in hand, their shoulders bumping. They carried their leftovers in their free hands. As they walked, Vincent tried to memorize the feel of her soft palm against his.

13

La Crosse, Wisconsin, October 2018

It had been okay, at first. They were mutually in pain, with twin sore hearts and matching exhaustion. But Vincent kept thinking, and thinking and thinking, and the more time that passed, the less he could see why they wouldn't work out. Li had offered that if he ever needed to talk things through again, she was there for him. It had nearly been a month, but he was still just as devastated. He hadn't talked to her in a couple of weeks. He had no idea how she was doing, and he was becoming paranoid that he'd imagined how important their week together had been.

Then he had a bad day. Got a grade back, not as high as he was expecting. He'd spent most of the previous weekend alone because his close buddies were out of town. He was spiraling, latching onto thoughts of Li when he needed to let go. But let go is not what happened.

It was a Tuesday evening. Vincent was lying on his back on his bed, his phone held over his head with both hands, a text written out but unsent. He shouldn't send it, he told himself, he should not send it. But he did. He first asked if her offer still stood, then if he could talk to her. She called him. His standard iPhone ringtone chirped for three seconds while he took a quick deep breath and answered.

"Hi, Vince," Li said. "How are you doing?"

"I'm . . . Are you sure it's okay to talk? I don't want to make you uncomfortable."

"If it is helpful for you to talk about how you're feeling, that is okay. I told you I'd be here for you as you need, and I meant it."

"Okay." There was a beat of silence as Vincent took another deep breath. And then he just started talking. "I can't see why we wouldn't work. I can't see it no matter how hard I try. We would still have all of this year, and next year. I am so upset over you, and we were only talking for a week. That's it. All of this might just be in my head, I don't know, maybe I'm giving that one week more value that it had, but I didn't know I could feel this way for another person and now that I do, I don't know what to do with myself. Li, please, tell me this isn't just in my head. That we could have a fighting chance. We ended over a future possibility, who knows what the future will bring. I can't—" Vincent sighed and pinched the bridge of his nose. "I just don't understand why we couldn't work."

"Vince . . . Wow." Li's voice was high-pitched, as if flustered, and sugary, not in pity but in kindness. "I—" There was a quick beat of static, probably from her taking a deep breath into the receiver. "To start, that week meant so much to me, too. That part is not just in your head. Don't think that. But I guess I was under the impression that us not continuing was a mutual decision."

Vincent let out an exasperated chuckle. "Yea, I'd thought so, too."

"The truth about people is that their cores rarely change," Li continued, in a soft, flowery voice. "Say we have the rest of this year, and next year. We fall in love. Then what? I'm going to stay here in the States. I want to live near my parents and grandparents, and so do my sisters. I could never live abroad, but it's your dream to live abroad. For us to work, one of us would have to sacrifice part of our core identity. That's not fair to either of us. Does that make more sense?"

"A little," Vincent whispered. The back of his mind was murmuring that his dreams could change someday. The future was yet untold. That line in the sand, he still couldn't see it. But Li explaining it in different ways wouldn't change anything. "Thank you, Li. I appreciate this."

"Of course, Vince. You're an amazing person. Don't forget that."

"You, too."

Li hung up. Vincent stared at the ceiling for a minute. Five. Ten. Until suddenly, he had his line in the sand. Li had told him no. He could hear it in her voice. She was done. Them yearning for one another was one thing, her turning him down was another. That was a line he could see, and no amount of fighting for her would ever change that. No, it would instead disrespect her, and he never wanted to do that.

Vincent started laugh-crying, silently and hysterically coughing, hugging himself, relieved he'd abruptly found closure, but devastated because he wanted hope.

14

New York City, March 2022

"Li was not my Great Heartbreak because we didn't work out," Vincent clarified. As he and Alice talked, they'd sunk further into the plush cushions. They each were deeply leaned into the back of the couch, watching the dining room as the first customers of the evening began trickling in. Mateo was shooting Vince warning glances as a couple customers stepped up to the bar, but Vincent ignored him. Alice was beginning to learn that Mateo was far more bark than bite.

"Li was the first time in my life that I saw a future where I wasn't alone," Vincent continued. "My mom was all I had, but even then, she was absent for much of my life while she worked hard to keep a roof over my head and put food on the table. Everything she did was for my benefit, and I love her endlessly for it. But with Li, for the first time, for that week, I had a partner. We were eating dinner together every night, talking for hours like it was minutes, and I suddenly had so much hope for a future that I would get to share with another person. It took time to untangle my very *mild*, romantic heartbreak from the devastating fear of being alone forever."

"I don't completely understand how you felt," Alice replied, "but I think I somewhat do. Fear of the future can be a powerful adversary."

Vincent sighed deeply. "Indeed it can."

"What brought you to Tranquility, then?" Alice asked.

Vincent blinked three times successively, rapidly, and said, "A couple months after that last conversation with Li, my mom got sick. I was her only family left, and she mine. She was okay at first, but over the summer, while I was home with her, I could tell that she was hiding how bad it actually was. I talked to my academic advisor, rushed through the last of my classes, graduated a semester early, then came home to take care of her." Vincent had laced his fingers together and was clenching them tightly, his knuckles going white. "By the time that she passed, nearly every penny had been spent on medical bills and hospice, including the money she'd been saving for me for law school. Her funeral took the rest of it." Vincent flung out his hand and stared Alice right in the eyes. "And don't get me wrong, I wouldn't have it any other way. My mom deserved those last few months of comfort, and then some."

He reclined back into the couch before continuing. "I sold all the furniture left in her apartment and used the money to move here. I couldn't stand to live in the place that she died. I'd had a buddy in college who moved here, and I spent a week crashing on his couch, spending it drunk or asleep. He kicked me out, I managed to get by on two part-time jobs and a crummy apartment until I stumbled upon Tranquility. Lilith hired me under the stipulation that she and Robin would help me invest and save for law school. I started working here about six months ago now, and I'm going to stay at least for another year and a half. In the fall of 2023, I'll start applying to law schools, and I'm scheduled to take the LSAT this summer."

"Do you still want to live in Europe?"

"Yes," Vincent replied immediately. "In the end, I never would have been able to give up living in Europe without also giving up a part of myself."

Alice pressed her lips together, and asked her final, self-motivated, question. "Do you have hope in your romantic future?"

Vincent hesitated this time. "Yes. It's hard to, but I know that one day, I'll have the power of hindsight, like I do now about what happened with Li. It's just a matter of living until then and appreciating my way there."

Alice spent the rest of that evening sitting on that plush couch, watching and listening. Vines broke through the carpet, growing through the ground, and wrapped around Alice's kitten-heeled boots. Their lithe limbs crawled cautiously across the toes of Alice's firmly flat-on-the-floor feet, then began creeping up her ankles.

Alice did not notice. She was watching the guests, in their evening dresses and tailored suits. A few of them flickered, as if their bodies were lampshades and buried within their intestines were twinkling lightbulbs. Dimming. Brightening.

After the show, when the dining room had cleared, Aunt Lilith emerged from backstage with a bright red feather boa wrapped around her neck. Alice stood up to go join her, but as she tried to pull her feet from the floor, the vines tugged against her, refusing to budge and begging her to stay. Alice crouched down. Her brow creased as she pressed her fingers against the latticework of thin vines. She used her fingernails to pry the vines away from her boots, but the vines started to grow around her fingers.

Then, suddenly, one by one, the vines snapped. Cut firmly in two.

"Ah, Harold likes you," Aunt Lilith said. She was standing in front of Alice, and she draped the feather boa across Alice's shoulders. The faux feathers tickled Alice's jaw.

"Harold?"

"The ghost cat." Lilith pointed to the snapped vines, which were rapidly retreating into the ground. "Kitten claws."

Smell The Flowers

3

15

New York City, March 2022

Alice was backstage, lounging on the plush, orange-leather couches with the singers. It was a late Sunday evening, nearing the early morning hours of Monday. During the dinner rush and performances, Alice helped Vincent carry trays of food out to the guests while intermittently sneaking glances at the singers onstage, eyeing their glittery or suede ensembles, wondering about their Great Heartbreaks.

Alice felt guilty for gobbling up others' heart-wrenching stories as entertainment. But that morning, Robin had been right about what this week was truly about. Hearing other heartbreak stories did make her feel less alone.

Lilith was the last to perform, with a cover of "I Will Always Love You" by Dolly Parton. Tonight, she wore a floor-length, tight-fitting, backless, black dress with butterfly sleeves. Once Lilith finished out the show, the customers in their suits and evening gowns filtered out, and Alice helped Vincent and Mateo wash the dishes.

Mateo had gone home to his family, and Vincent and Alice sank back into their earlier couch while they babbled about college professors and exorbitant textbook prices.

Nearing midnight, Lilith peered through the curtains onstage. She pushed the center seam apart and stepped half-through, then beckoned Alice backstage. "You're both welcome to join!" Lilith yelled across the empty dining room, so that Vincent and Alice could hear her from where they sat against the back wall.

"I think I'll head to bed," Vincent yawned, quietly, to Alice. "Let Lilith know she did great tonight."

"Sure."

Now, Alice was backstage, on the end of one of those bright-colored couches in the vanity-light-lit space, her lap draped with a scratchy wool blanket. All five singers were there. Josiah, Enid, Max, Carmela. They had reintroduced themselves when Alice first joined them, and Alice had spent the succeeding fifteen minutes doing her best to memorize their names while the group bantered and laughed about the state of Enid's friend's roommate's love life.

Alice was glancing at each of them in order, memorizing, Josiah, Enid, Lilith, Max, Carmela, when Lilith said, "Okay, I think we've tortured Alice enough with talking about someone she doesn't know."

"Agreed," Carmela said quickly, "and I would like to volunteer to share my Great Heartbreak first." There was a chorus of groans. "If no one objects?"

"You're always first," Josiah frowned.

"Oh, let her have it!" Max said. They stood, still wrapped up in their blanket, and shuffled toward the dining room. "I'll see y'all tomorrow."

"Oh, fine!" Josiah conceded. He stood, rested a hand on Alice's shoulder, and said, "We'll talk tomorrow, dear."

There was a chorus of "Goodbyes" and "Goodnights" until it was just Lilith, Carmela, and Alice on the couches.

"I'll go make tea," Lilith said, then shuffled off as well.

"It's nice to formally meet you, Alice," Carmela said.

Carmela had deep gold skin and walnut-brown hair cut into a long pixie. She was wearing a bright red A-line dress with a high-low hem, and the dress billowed across the arm of the couch. She was sipping on a Shirley Temple slowly. She wore deep red lipstick that left marks on her glass, and she kept swiping a finger around the edge of her lips to check if the lipstick had smeared.

"My Great Heartbreak can be summed up into, 'It is okay to be single,'" Carmela laughed. She had dainty crow's feet below her eyes and a gap between her two front teeth, noticeable only because of her continuous, genuine grinning. "But if you'd like to hear the full story, I'd be happy to tell you."

"I would," Alice said.

Carmela grinned again. Her temples were the rosy red of chrysanthemums, and sunflowers bloomed behind her eyes.

16

Madison, Wisconsin, September 2003

Carmela Flores was clutching Carter Young's hand like a lifeline. They were sitting side by side on a wooden bench facing Lake Mendota. The sun was setting, and the temperature was dipping into the fifties. Carmela shivered in her jeans and thin, dark green T-shirt, but Carter was solid, firm, the anchor to Carmela's trembling.

They'd been together for a year. Just.

"I think we're growing apart," Carter said. He stared off at the lake, at the rippling water, yet squeezing Carmela's hand back in kind. "We *are* growing apart. Do you feel it, too?"

Carmela let the silence hang for a moment, knowing in her gut what her answer was. She nodded her head and said, "Yes, I do."

Carter had been her first boyfriend. They met as soon as they arrived at the University of Wisconsin-Madison as freshman, and they'd been together since. Sure, things hadn't been the *best* as of late. They were both busy with classes and wouldn't see one another during the week. Their calendars were empty of future plans. But they cared about one another, and the busyness would end, eventually. Probably.

"So, what now?" Carter asked. He finally turned to look at Carmela. His green eyes were cloudy with tears.

"Well." Carmela hiccup-sobbed once, and said, "I think you're my ex now. And I'm yours."

They were still gripping palms, his soft skin against her dry skin, clenching tightly, knowing that they had to let go.

17

MADISON, WISCONSIN, OCTOBER 2003

His name was Maddox. He had scruffy blond hair and a tattoo of an asymmetrical, black-and-white monarch butterfly that his older brother had dared him to get on his twenty-first birthday, and he'd been too drunk to realize it was a bad idea. He batted his eyelashes sensually and squeezed Carmela's waist too tight when he kissed her.

He'd asked her out three weeks to the day of her break-up with Carter. Carmela said yes.

Maddox took her out for ice cream. They split a chocolate raspberry sundae with extra whip cream, extra chocolate syrup, and added butterscotch, making it one of the most expensive items on the menu. When they went to pay, Maddox had forgotten his wallet, so Carmela pulled a few crumpled bills from her fraying wallet.

They lasted two weeks before Maddox lost interest. Carmela was too studious.

18

MADISON, WISCONSIN, NOVEMBER 2003

His name was Harrison. He had close-cropped black hair and wore fatigues or sweaters with khakis. He was one of the ROTC students.

Carmela met him at church. She'd started going again, filling the free time she suddenly had. He liked the way she smiled, so open-mouthed, so gap-toothed. It was endearing. He took her out for a pizza dinner, but when she leaned in to kiss him goodnight, he took a step backward. "Not yet," he'd said.

They lasted three weeks, most of November, and finally, on that last week, they kissed. Harrison broke it off the next night. Carmela wasn't religious enough.

19

MADISON, WISCONSIN, DECEMBER 2003

His name was Jack. He had an abundance of freckles on his nose, shoulders, arms. Carmela met him at the library, when they shared a table the week before finals. He asked for her number, she said yes.

They lasted one date. They went out for dinner on a Saturday evening, and when Carmela asked him out again the next day, he said he couldn't go out on a Sunday night. Not on a school night.

20

Madison, Wisconsin, January 2004

His name was Marco.

21

Madison, Wisconsin, February 2004

His name was—

22

NEW YORK CITY, MARCH 2022

"In the eight-month span after Carter and I broke up, I had eight different love interests," Carmela concluded, drinking the last of her Shirley Temple. "It was to the detriment of my self-worth. I jumped from man to man, never pausing once to find validation from myself. Take my story as a cautionary tale. Be single until *you* are ready for a relationship, not until the next guy falls out of the sky." Carmela smiled her teeth-baring smile at Alice, leaned forward on the couch and reached out to take Alice's hand, then said, "Remember. There will always be men."

It was nearing one in the morning, and Alice's eyes were burning. By the end of her story, Carmela was yawning, too. Lilith's tea had only calmed them further, and Lilith's blatant snoring as she reclined on the couch beside Carmela wasn't helping, either. But there was something about staying up late, talking into the night, that made the words exchanged more powerful, more meaningful.

Maybe Lilith's ooey-gooey life-changing nonsense was messing with Alice's brain.

Carmela glanced up at the clock and shook her head. "It is entirely too late." She stood, found a blanket, and gently draped it over Lilith. Carmela's dress trailed her like water dripping from a swimsuit after stepping out of a pool. "Lilith'll be okay here tonight. I'll crash in one of the guest rooms."

Carmela walked with Alice through the dining room, to the flowered hallway, and she bid her goodnight before stepping through a door painted vermillion. Alice returned to her room, to the rumpled bed she hadn't bothered to make up.

If she were at her dorm, she would have slept fitfully, the heartbreaks of Lilith, Mateo, Vince, Carmela, and herself muddling her dreams, but she was at Tranquility, and as she breathed deeply, evenly, the flowers in the hall rose and fell with her chest. Alice slept calmly until mid-afternoon the next day.

Alice woke up Monday afternoon—around a respectable two-thirty—to find a tray of oatmeal, granola, vanilla yogurt, and a well-loved, spine-broken paperback of *Pride and Prejudice* waiting outside her bedroom door. After a warm shower and settling on distressed jeans and an emerald-green sweater, Alice wandered out to the dining room, settled into one of the peripheral couches, and started reading. She made sure to keep her feet tucked up onto the couch.

Josiah would be joining her after he performed, and Alice read in the meantime. The book had markings in the margins, stars and exclamation marks and hearts, and text underlined. Written on the bottom of a page was, "Life would be better if we all listened."

Around nine-thirty in the evening, Josiah stepped out from backstage.

He was an older man in his sixties or seventies. He had gray hair and laugh lines around his eyes, and he was wearing a navy-blue suit, but the jacket was draped over his arm and he'd rolled the sleeves of his white, button-down up to his elbows to expose forearms of swirling, black-and-white floral tattoos. He sat beside Alice on the couch. The cushion dipped to cradle him.

"Hello, Alice," Josiah said softly. "How has Tranquility treated you so far?"

Alice stuck a bookmark—a ripped-off corner from the envelope of Lilith's letter—into *Pride and Prejudice* and rotated on the couch so that she was facing Josiah. "It's been emotionally stimulating to say the least," she said.

"Ha! I know what you mean." Josiah leaned back into the couch. "I've been here *almost* as long as Lilith, and life with Lilith is always eventful. Would you like to wait for Lilith to join before I start?"

Alice glanced upward, to the stage where Lilith was adjusting the microphone. "No, that's okay."

"Lilith has heard this story hundreds of times, anyways."

23

St. Louis, Missouri, April 1998

Josiah Sanders was walking down a busy city street, toward Francis Park, a brown paper bag clutched in his hands. Within were two peanut butter and jelly sandwiches, a jar of pickles, an overripe apple, an underripe orange, a resealable bag of carrot sticks, two freshly cut petunias, and a love letter.

It was Josiah and his partner's twenty-fifth anniversary. They'd first met in kindergarten, in Cleveland, Ohio, back in 1960, in Mrs. Hinkley's class. Charles had pretended to be allergic to peanut butter sandwiches so the teacher wouldn't make him sit next to Josiah, who had a habit of 'borrowing' food items from his classmates' lunches. Their lives parted when Charles' family moved to upstate New York the following year, but Charles and Josiah's paths crossed again here, in St. Louis, at Francis Park.

Josiah was on his lunch break, sitting on a bench, feeding ducks the crust from his peanut butter and jelly sandwich, when Charles, who had just moved there for a new job opportunity and was exploring the city, spotted him. They didn't recognize one another at first. Josiah was wearing a Cleveland Browns baseball cap, a quick fashion accessory to keep the sun out of his eyes that he'd on occasion forget to take off before heading back in to work and that clashed fantastically with his blue, well-tailored suit. Charles saw it, and in want of friends, struck up a conversation.

In the ensuing months, they realized their Mrs. Hinkley connection, and eventually fell in love and moved in together. They didn't have an official anniversary, never formally asking one another to be their partner, so they celebrated the day that they moved in together with a picnic lunch of peanut butter and jelly sandwiches in Francis Park—Charles quite liked a well-made peanut butter sandwich, and wasn't a bit allergic, which Josiah thought was the cleverest thing in the world.

That year, the year of their twenty-fifth picnic, Josiah arrived at Francis Park first. He found an empty bench—unfortunately not the one they met at, though sometimes on anniversary days, it was available—and sat down. He set the brown paper bag on his lap and waited.

Waited.

Waited.

As Josiah waited, his stomach clenching uneasily, he didn't know that Charles had gotten out of a meeting late. That Charles was rushing over, a love letter of his own tucked into his suit jacket. That Charles started walking through a crosswalk that only had three seconds left, and a car turning right didn't yield.

That as the jelly in their sandwiches soaked into the porous bread, Charles' blood soaked into the concrete of the street.

24

St. Louis, Missouri, December 1999

Josiah was sitting in his apartment on New Year's Eve with all the lights off. The TV was on, set to the broadcast from Times Square. The ball was going to drop in thirty minutes, it was nearly a new century. Well, in the eastern time zone. Josiah had another hour to spare.

The apartment was disorganized but clean. Josiah hand-washed all his dishes as soon as he used them and put all dirty clothes in the hamper. The floors were scrubbed, the counters wiped down. But there were knickknacks everywhere. After Charles passed, every memento, every scrap of memorabilia from over the years, was brought out, framed or cleaned, set out on cheaply bought shelves and tables. Photographs from date nights, T-shirts from short vacations. The apartment had become a shrine to Charles.

Josiah didn't have anyone over anymore. A few friends initially expressed concern over Josiah's shelf building, and Josiah hadn't invited them back since.

But now, here he was, sitting alone, on New Year's Eve, surrounded by artifacts of the man he still deeply loved, and for the first time was questioning whether grasping on so tightly had been healthy.

Josiah turned the TV volume up louder and stood to get a Pepsi from the fridge. The entryway was in direct view of the kitchen, and as Josiah tugged open the refrigerator door, he glanced down the hallway, at the bundle of Charles' clothes that the hospital had given him the day that he died. It had been set by the front door and left there. Had been there for over a year.

Josiah forgot the Pepsi. Closed the door. Walked toward the bundle. Crouched down. Reached trembling hands into the bag. Pulled out Charles' suitcoat. Dropped it. It was stained with blood.

Out from the coat fluttered Charles' love letter, pristine and sealed as if he had licked it closed yesterday. *"Josiah Sanders"* and a heart were written on the envelope. With tears dripping down Josiah's cheeks, he picked up the precious letter and hurried to the kitchen, to flip on a light and grab a letter opener. The envelope sliced open cleanly, and Josiah pulled out cream paper. He started reading.

"My love," the letter started, in Charles' linear handwriting, *"happy anniversary. Here is to the twenty-five years of our lives we have spent together, to the memories we've made and to our love. But here is also to the twenty-five more years, God willing, that we will get to spend together. I could wax poetic about how I feel for you, but this year, I'm not going to do that. Inside this envelope you'll find two plane tickets to New York City, two tickets for* Phantom of the Opera *and two tickets for* Chicago. *I know you've dreamed of adventuring beyond Missouri and the Midwest, and I can't*

think of a better way to experience the world than to travel it with you. Happy anniversary. Affectionately yours, Charles."

Inside the envelope were the six total tickets, scheduled for last year's December. Winter in New York. Christmas in New York. Josiah was openly weeping now, tears pitter-pattering on the letter, once again mourning the future that he and Charles would never have.

Josiah read and reread the letter until the ball dropped, until it was midnight in St. Louis. A sense of calm was invading his bloodstream, as he suddenly had clarity of what this letter meant, and what Charles was trying to tell him. It was time to go. It was time to leave St. Louis. Whatever Josiah did, Charles would be with him every step of the way, not hiding in memorabilia.

It was time to move to New York.

25

New York City, February 2000

Josiah was walking through Manhattan, his new shoes pinching his toes and leaving blisters on his heels, the front of his shirt and chest hair beneath smeared with spilled black coffee. In his pocket, now with a couple more stains on its pages, was the anniversary letter from Charles. A few coffee stains weren't devastating—Josiah had nearly put the letter through the wash a couple weeks ago. Charles was always the one to remind Josiah to check his pants pockets before washing his clothes.

Then. There, a woman was crying. More rather, weeping. She was standing outside a squat building stuffed between a drugstore and an alleyway, her hand pressed flat against a bright red front door. Her head was thrown back, and a river of strawberry-blonde curls dripped down her back. She was open-mouthed as she cried. From her eyes leaked tears streaked with mascara.

Josiah had to walk right past her. Normally, he'd cross the street. Get away from this woman's cloud of pain. But traffic was too thick to dart across the street, and as Josiah neared the woman, he asked, "Are you alright?"

The woman turned her head. Josiah was close enough to see the rivulets of mascara-contaminated tears and clear snot in her foundation. The woman cleared her throat and said in a raspy, swollen voice, "I have never been so overjoyed and devastated at the same time." The woman retracted her hand from the door and pressed her palm against her heart. "You understand."

Charles' letter in his pocket. Josiah did understand.

The fly-buzz of the tattoo gun fluttered through the air of the tattoo parlor. Josiah had his arm outstretched, a needle threading black ink into his forearm, petunias steadily emerging on his skin. Lilith clutched Josiah's hand and murmured the occasional encouragement, but Josiah couldn't hear her.

Josiah was too focused on the phantom fingers on his shoulder, squeezing tight enough to say, "I'm okay. You're okay now, too."

26

New York City, March 2022

"I had just moved into a tiny studio apartment in Manhattan when I met Lilith," Josiah concluded, absentmindedly rubbing the swirling floral tattoos on his forearm with his thumb. "She'd opened Tranquility the week prior, and she invited me in for a drink on the house. I came back every night after, and I've kept coming back, all these years."

"I would keep coming back, too," Alice said.

Josiah chuckled. "I'm glad you think so, but at the end of this week, you should leave and not come back."

Alice's brow furrowed. "Why not? Everyone is so welcoming and kind here."

"We will always be here, to listen to you as you need, but staying here is for those that are at the end of their journey, or at a pause, like Vince. You are nineteen with a whole life ahead of you. *Go live it*."

As they'd been talking, the vines had grown again, breaking through the carpet and wrapping around Josiah's dress shoes. "It was a pleasure to talk to you,"

Josiah said, "And I'll see you around." Josiah stood and nodded at Alice, and just as Alice was about to point out the vines, Josiah stepped out of them as easily as a knife slicing through room temperature butter. They snapped, wilted, then shrank back into the carpet.

Alice stared at the carpet, at where the vines should have been, and whispered, "Harold?" There was no reply.

Tuesday morning brought French toast, candied strawberries, chocolate milk, and *A Tree Grows in Brooklyn* by Betty Smith. Alice spent the morning in bed finishing off *Pride and Prejudice,* then climbed into a pair of patchwork jeans and a creamy-white sweater to carry her breakfast tray to the kitchen behind the bar and meet Lilith for lunch.

Alice and Lilith were dining on frozen green grapes and grilled turkey-and-cheese sandwiches, sitting at one of the pristine-white tablecloth tables. "Your mom *tried* to get revenge," Lilith was saying, her face scrunched up with laughter, "but when she went to find my baby pictures, I'd gotten to them first!"

"It's nice to hear stories of Mom as a kid," Alice said, wiping the corners of her mouth with a napkin that matched the tablecloth. "It's nice to hear stories about Mom at *all*. She doesn't talk about before Edith and I were born, not even a little. When we ask her what high school was like, or about college, and falling in love with Dad, she gives us cop out answers. About how great it was, or how she just knew dad was The One and that was that."

"Your mom has her reasons," Lilith said.

Alice shrugged her shoulders. "I guess. It just would be nice to know *something* about my mom when she wasn't . . . before she was my mom. And with Dad, too."

Lilith rested her hand on Alice's shoulder and rubbed Alice's collarbone with her thumb. "Your mom loves you, and she's trying to raise you the best she knows. She wants to be a mother you look up to and respect."

"I do respect her! I also feel like I don't really know her." Alice sighed and popped a frozen grape in her mouth. "Why haven't you come to visit us more often? I know Edith would love to see you."

"Oh," Lilith sighed, her smile falling from her face. "Your mom and I love one another *endlessly*, never forget that." She wagged a pointer finger in the air as she said this. "But. We have different visions and goals about how to live our lives, and that's okay. Your mom has her stable, suburban life, with her average of two kids, and a successful, dependable career. When you were born, and then your sister, your mom kept looking at me, silently wondering when I'd have what she had found, when I'd have my own kids that could be best friends with her kids, but that's not how I see my life. Being around your mom, and her disappointment, though she tries to hide it, can be taxing. That's why I haven't been around you girls as much as I should have been."

Alice reached across the table, her palm outstretched, and Lilith put her hand in Alice's. Alice squeezed once, tightly, then let go, and she didn't say anything.

Enid was a woman in her mid-fifties, both curvy and willowy, with dark brown skin and tightly curled hair that fell just past her shoulders. She was wearing a bulky, black sweatshirt and bright red leggings, despite performing a melancholy ballad in a stunning, hip-hugging, fishtail, honey-yellow dress a mere thirty minutes before sitting down with Alice.

They were sitting at one of the tables in the dining room, in the back corner. The table was draped in a creamy, cotton tablecloth with a vase of irises and two lilac-colored candles in the center.

"My Great Heartbreak isn't about my love life," Enid said. She was leaning forward, her elbows on the table, her chin resting on laced together fingers. "I've been with my wife for thirty years now. We only married about seven years ago, back in 2015, but we've been together since grad school." A whimsy look passed over her. "She was my first kiss, if you'll believe it."

"That's so romantic."

Enid shook her head and cleared her throat. "But our love story is one for another night. Now, my Great Heartbreak."

27

Los Angeles, California, June 1986

Enid Anderson had three part-time jobs that summer of '86. She worked for the post office in the early morning hours, worked retail at Goodwill during the day, and had evening shifts at a pizza parlor not too far from her family's home in Northridge. She wore jeans and a light blue T-shirt to her first two jobs, swapping a different apron for each establishment, and had time between Goodwill and the pizza parlor to head home, change into her uniform and eat something, then off she went.

Enid had graduated high school a month prior and had leapt from a busy school schedule to a busy work schedule. She'd worked before, but nothing like this. The meager savings she had had in her bank account had doubled by the end of May.

With every package she arranged on the correct shelf, with every Goodwill customer she directed to the correct section of the store, with every pizza pie she cooked to a crispy, golden brown, she grew more excited for college. She was going to California State University there in Los Angeles, intending to become a nurse. Every penny saved was a penny toward books and tuition.

Her parents were going to help as much as they were able, but Enid knew not to expect more than a few meager checks toward tuition. Which was okay. She was the eldest, and she'd rather her parents save for her siblings. Ingrid was dreaming of being an astronaut that lived on the moon, Arthur an engineer that would help get her there, and John a paleontologist that dug up dinosaurs.

Her family's home was just big enough to hold all of them. Enid shared a bedroom with her little sister, Ingrid, and her little brothers, Arthur and John, shared another, with their parents claiming the last bedroom. All the children had to share one bathroom. Being up before all her siblings meant the bathroom was hers for the taking, which Enid quite liked.

It was Sunday, her one day off. Enid and her siblings were in the kitchen, sitting around their scuffed, oakwood table, watching their father make chocolate-chip waffles for breakfast while their mom was upstairs, ironing the wrinkles out of their clothes. The air smelled of chocolate, rich and sweet, soaking pleasantly into their pores.

"Dad, can I go first?" John asked.

"No, can I go first?" Arthur said.

"What about me?" Ingrid added.

The three of them, though in late elementary school and middle school, pushed their chairs back violently and raced to the cupboard, each reaching for a plate and dashing for a place 'in line' to their dad's right.

"Woah, woah, woah!" their dad said, just as he pulled the first two chocolate-chip waffles off the rectangular waffle maker. "I think Enid should get the first waffle."

"No, not fair!" and "Youngest first!" they chorused comically, not actually upset by this.

"Thank you, Dad," Enid said, as he took one of the clean plates from Enid's brothers, then gingerly set one waffle on it for Enid and gave the second waffle to Ingrid.

Within a few minutes, all four children were sitting around the kitchen table, eating their waffles, getting sticky syrup on their fingers and the corners of their mouths.

"We're going to miss you," Ingrid said, once she'd finished her waffle. The thought of Enid leaving for college had been hanging over the children's heads like impending rainclouds ever since Enid committed to California State. It had a habit of popping up during their happy moments, especially for Ingrid.

"I'm not going far," Enid replied, pulling Ingrid in for a side hug with her arm, holding her hand aloft to keep syrup away from Enid's pink, fuzzy pajamas.

"She can come home for chocolate-chip waffles on Sunday, if she'd like!" their dad said as he started washing their dirty dishes, scrubbing a deep blue cloth against puddled syrup.

Ingrid pressed her lips together and didn't say anything else; she didn't understand why Enid couldn't just live at home and commute. It would be cheaper. Their family could stay together.

"Come get dressed!" their mom hollered from upstairs. There was a thundering of footsteps as the children hurried up the stairs, collected their slacks and button downs and dresses from their mom, then to their rooms to change. There was a shuffling of feet as they trampled back down the stairs. A standard family Sunday morning.

Except.

John slipping on the top stair in his dress socks and his soft, mewing cry as he landed on his arm at the bottom was not typical of their morning ambiance. Nor was his wailing as he clutched an elbow bent the wrong direction.

28

Los Angeles, California, August 1986

On the way back from her last shift of the summer, Enid stopped by the grocery store to buy a teddy bear for John. It was the first of her wages that she'd spent. She had a little cash on her at all times, and in her wallet were the checks for her last paychecks. She'd use the cash to buy the teddy bear tonight and go in the morning to deposit the checks into her account.

The teddy bear was light blue, John's favorite color, with a cream, oval belly, and had a big white bow with the words, "Feel better soon," written in blue, blocky letters. Poor John had had a rough summer. His fall required arm surgery, and instead of digging out in the dirt searching for dinosaur bones as he had envisioned this summer, he spent it in hospital beds and in his room.

Enid made it home around ten and crept quietly upstairs. Her brothers' bedroom door was ajar, and she peeked through the seam. John and Arthur were deep in sleep, snoring on opposite intervals of one other. Enid smiled to herself, then tucked the teddy bear under her arm. She'd give it to him in the morning.

Ingrid was in bed, reading *Two Fables* by Roald Dahl by the light of a lamp on their shared nightstand. "You're still up?" Enid asked. She fished through her closet for pajamas, finding a pair of light blue sweatpants and an oversized T-shirt with the words, "Debate Club Champions 1984" across the front in white bubble letters.

"I wanted to see you," Ingrid said, putting her book away. "You're leaving in a few days."

Enid didn't reply. She climbed into her bed. They had two twin beds pushed against the walls of their room, with pale yellow comforters their mom had made from curtains she found at a Salvation Army. "Could I sleep with you tonight?" Ingrid asked softly.

Enid pushed herself as close to the wall as she could get, then pushed her comforter aside. "Sure." The two sisters wrapped their arms around one another and slept, the elder dreaming of what lay in her future and the younger dreading the days to come.

Enid arrived at the bank early that next morning, checks in hand. After this, her balance would be above $7,000! Between graduation gifts, saving her money from previous birthdays and jobs, and her summer of working around eighty-hour weeks, she would have more than enough for her first semester.

"Your current balance is $538.24," the bank teller said.

"What?"

"Your current balance is $538.24," the bank teller repeated.

"I thought I had over $7,000." Enid's heart was thumping erratically, and her palms started sweating.

The bank teller disappeared behind the counter, then reappeared and said, "There was a large withdrawal a couple weeks ago."

"I haven't made any withdrawals." Enid's breath was catching, and she struggled to draw air through her nose.

"Are there any other account owners?"

Enid blinked a few times. "My dad's a co-owner," she replied flatly.

When her dad got home from work that night, Enid waited until after dinner, after her siblings had gone upstairs to fight over who brushed their teeth first, to approach her dad.

"Hey, honey, do you need something?" he asked. He was washing the dinner dishes, wearing gloves in the steaming water, while Enid's mom had a dish towel, was drying the clean dishes, and putting them back in the cupboards.

"I went to the bank today, and the teller said—"

"Look, honey," her mom started saying. Her parents' eyes darted back and forth, making eye contact, then away.

Her dad turned off the sink and took off his gloves, took a deep breath. "We needed it for John's surgery," he admitted. He wouldn't meet Enid's eyes. "We're going to pay you back. Every penny."

Enid stared at the ground, knowing full well that even if her parents did pay her back, it would take years. The money she needed for school wasn't going to magically appear before the first bill was due. Enid rubbed her temples with her fingers and sighed. "Okay," she said. Enid had resolved herself to silence. It was silence or screaming, crying, weeping.

"We're so sorry, honey." Enid turned to leave, but her parents kept saying, "We're sorry," over and over.

"You know," Enid whispered, with her back to her parents. Their apologies silenced, "if you had asked me for the money, I probably would have given it to you. But you didn't ask."

"Honey, we're so sorry," her dad said again.

"I'd like my birth certificate. And my social security card." Her father stared at her, his eyes wide and hands outstretched, reaching for her. "Right now."

Their brows creased, but her mom said, "Okay."

Enid went upstairs. Started packing for college, shoving away everything she owned, her clothes, her few favorite paperback books, her birth certificate and social security card, into two cardboard boxes. She left out a small duffel bag, with her toiletries and enough clothes to last her a few days. The next morning, Enid called her future roommate at CSU and asked if she could store a couple boxes in her garage until they moved in, and the roommate agreed. That afternoon she went to the bank, withdrew the remaining $538.24 from her account, opened her own account, one without her father joint on it, and took out a loan to pay for her first semester.

On the day she moved out, Enid wrapped each of her siblings in a tight bear hug. The last person she said goodbye to was her father. "You're always welcome to come for Sunday morning waffles," he said.

"I'll come as often as I can," Enid said. "But not for you," in a quieter voice. She motioned to her siblings with an outstretched palm. "For them."

29

New York City, March 2022

The customers had all left, and the dining room was once again still and quiet. Mateo had brought Alice and Enid dishes of mango sherbet, and their empty bowls and used spoons were sitting on the table, beneath the irises.

"I lost both of my parents that day," Enid said, "and our relationship has never been the same. Not with my siblings, either. All they saw was that I never came back, except to visit. I don't think they know what happened, and I don't want them to." Enid sighed. "John would be devastated if he knew."

"What became of all of you?" Alice asked.

"Well, Ingrid became an aerospace engineer, got married. I have a couple nieces. They live in Texas, now. Arthur became a barber, opened up his own business in LA, and is living close to our parents. John is living in Europe at different archaeological digs but finding pottery instead of dinosaurs. I don't know if that makes him happy or if he's disappointed. We don't talk anymore."

"And you're here at Tranquility."

"Well, yes," Enid laughed. "But I'm also a nurse. So is my wife. We work the first shift. If you have any interest in being a nurse, we'd love to have you interview us, or job shadow one of us."

Alice's nose scrunched before she could help herself, and Enid started laughing. "The medical field doesn't call to me," Alice said, "but thank you for the offer."

Enid glanced around the empty dining room. "I should get going. Monday night is movie night. My love is waiting for me."

"I can take the dirty dishes back," Alice offered.

"Thank you."

The women parted, Alice back toward the bar and the kitchen, Enid toward the hallway. A petal from an iris fell from the stem and rested on the table.

Alice was in her borrowed room, sprawled across the bed, with her cell phone in her hand. On the screen was her mom's contact card. The profile picture was a selfie lifted from her mom's Facebook page the last time her mom dyed her hair to chestnut brown. It was near midnight in New York, but it was only nine back home. Her mom should still be awake.

Alice clicked the call button and pressed her phone to her ear, breathing in and out in time to the dial tone.

"Hi, Allie!"

"Hi, Mom."

"How has your break been? Your dad and I have been worried about you!"

"It's been really nice to see Aunt Lilith again." Alice held her breath, afraid that if she breathed as heavy as her beating heart wanted her to, the receiver would crackle and her mom wouldn't be able to hear her. "Mom, can I ask you a question?"

"Sure, sweets."

"Can you tell me about you and Dad? Like, how you met and why you got married and life before Edith and me?"

"Oh, you know the story! Your dad and I are high school sweethearts, we got married right after college, and we had you—"

"No, Mom, that's not what I mean."

Ellie sighed into the phone, then whispered, "Your aunt and her Great Heartbreaks."

Alice let the silence settle for a couple minutes before asking, "Have you visited Tranquility before?"

"Once." The line went quiet as Alice's mom collected her thoughts. "I came out to visit a few months before I found out I was pregnant with you. I came by myself. It'd been nearly four years since I'd seen my sister, and she invited me to stay for a long weekend. I got pickpocketed walking back from a used bookstore. Thief took my wallet, but not the books. I'd found *Pride and Prejudice* and *The Virgin Suicides* in pretty good condition, I think. Or maybe it was *Emma* and *The Giver*. I forget . . . But I never did get my wallet back, it was made of real—"

"Mom, I feel like I can't talk to you about the important things because *you* don't talk to *me* about the important things." Silence. "Mom?" Alice could faintly hear her mom's breath through the static.

"My sister will tell the world all the ways that she isn't perfect, and I can't do that."

Alice curled up on the bed, slouching onto her side and pulling her knees to her chest. "But I'm your daughter. Shouldn't we be able to talk to one another about anything?"

Over the phone, there was the click of footsteps, then creaking door hinges and a door latching closed. "Your dad and I are high school sweethearts," Ellie said in a low voice. "He asked me to prom—"

"No! Mom!" Alice interrupted. "Not this *again*, the short, fake-happy answers—"

"Listen!" Ellie hissed. "Just . . . listen." A sigh trickled through the line. "James asked me to prom," Ellie continued, "and I got his friend to ask Lils, so she could help me. Lils always knew more than me about romance and how to get a guy to like you back, and without Lils, I don't know if your dad and I would have even started dating. Then Lils graduated and went off to college, and Mom—your grandma—didn't talk about romance or sex or birth control, and I didn't have Lils there to look out for me anymore. My senior year of high school, I got pregnant. I remember buying the pregnancy test at the drugstore after school, then James pacing back and forth in front of his superhero posters in his bedroom as we waited for the result. He drove back home from college as soon as I told him I was going to take a test." Breathy laughter cut across the line. "We took his mom's tomato-shaped kitchen timer to wait out the results. As soon as it came back positive, James didn't say a word, just told me to get in his car. He drove me to a pawn shop and pointed at their ring display and said, 'Will you marry me?' I picked a gold ring with a tiny emerald—who knows if it was real gold and emerald, I've never had it appraised—then wore it on a silver chain around my neck under my clothes for five weeks. The night before we were going to tell our parents about the baby and our engagement, I miscarried."

Ellie was crying now, her words punctuated with soft hiccups. "I called Lils and told her everything," she continued, "then Lils helped me get on birth control. James proposed with a diamond ring—the ring I've always worn during our marriage—a couple years later. I graduated college, we got married, then started trying for a baby. I miscarried three more times before I got pregnant with Clara May. I was so cautious during the pregnancy. I stopped working, I spent all of my time in bed. I carried her for a full nine months and then—then she—she was stillborn." Ellie's voice was growing steadily higher-pitched and faster. "Grief can take its toll on a marriage. Your dad and I nearly divorced, a couple years after we lost Clara May."

"Oh, Mom," Alice murmured. There was nothing else she could think to say.

"We never told you or Edith about Clara May because it was so incredibly painful for us, for me, that I can't talk about her, or I think about what life would look like if she were still in it. Having you was a miracle, sweets, and Edith, too. I'm sorry that I haven't been there for you when you needed me through the hard emotions. I'm here for you, sweets, I'm here to listen. Tell me about Rylan."

"I will, Mom," Alice said. "Not right now, I can't right now, but I will."

"Okay, sweets, whenever you're ready. Just talk to me."

The two women stayed on the line for another ten minutes, listening to one another breathe in and out over the phone. Vines had broken through the carpet, crept up the bedframe, and were weaving a tapestry across the ceiling. Purring permeated the air, and pitter-patter paw prints padded across the mattress, waiting for Alice to fall asleep and the vines to recede like dandelion seeds drifting away in the wind.

The Yellow, White, and Red Chrysanthemums

4

30

NEW YORK CITY, MARCH 2022

On Wednesday, Tranquility was closed.

"Wednesday is the hardest day of the week," Lilith had lamented over dinner Tuesday night. "We don't make the day more difficult than need be."

Alice spent the morning and early afternoon reading *A Tree Grows in Brooklyn* while gnawing on an entire loaf of sourdough bread that she had found outside her room that morning. Alice was pointedly ignoring her backpack of schoolwork. The longer Alice spent in her room, the longer her unwritten Lit essay crept into her conscious, so Alice took *A Tree Grows in Brooklyn* out to the reception area.

Max was there, sitting in one of the rocking chairs, staring out the front window. They had shoulder-length, golden hair, and brown freckles across the pale skin of their nose, and they were wearing a well-tailored black suit with a pale blue, button-down undershirt. They had a notebook open on their lap and were writing on a half-filled page with a bright purple pen.

"Oh!" Max said when they noticed Alice standing in the doorway, her book haphazardly hanging out of her hand. "Hi, Alice."

"Hi, Max. Is it okay if I join you?"

"Of course." Max turned back to their notebook while Alice made herself comfortable on the couch. Max was the only singer Alice hadn't officially met one-on-one yet. Alice tucked the envelope-corner-turned-bookmark amongst the later pages of the book and began halfheartedly reading, almost expecting Max to start talking. Waiting in anticipation.

"Lilith calls our stories our Great Heartbreak," Max said, breaking the comfortable silence yet still writing in their notebook, "but, really, they're all just tragedies, and part of being human. Has it been difficult, hearing everyone's tragedies?"

"Yes," Alice said immediately. "And no." She didn't elaborate. She didn't know how to.

"Well," Max sighed, "You can stop waiting. I'm not going to tell you my tragedy. I've just met you, and I don't know you. I don't owe you vulnerability. Lilith doesn't believe in that philosophy, but I think that's why I'm here. To balance her out. Robin would be in the middle of us, I would say, with his stance on the Great Heartbreaks."

"I understand," Alice said, though she couldn't help but feel a bit miffed. Every other person had been open and trusting, but then, at the thought of being forced to tell others, telling strangers, about her break-up story without knowing them at all, she *did* understand.

Telling them about begging Rylan to spend time with her. About his digital calendar, and time with her outlined in flamingo-pink blocks. About Rylan tucking pink into spare minutes, filling his weekends with as much Alice as he could. Until the proportion of pink shrunk by minutes. Seconds. Days. Telling them about pleading for a kiss. About pleading for Rylan's awkward, open-mouthed kisses. About his calloused fingertips. Telling them about waiting to not be so exhausted by being with him, about the days filled with useless pining.

Telling a stranger about what Rylan had said to her, the night they broke up.

Alice understood Max perfectly.

"Watch the glass with me," Max said. They pointed at the window, the one facing the bustling Manhattan street. It was late afternoon, and groups of people hurried down the sidewalks, both the one directly in front of Tranquility and the one across the street. The people's faces were blurred in the glass, yet their bodies, clothing, and shoes were luminescent and clear. Most of the figures passing by outside had wings jutting from their backs, from their shoulder blades. Dove wings, butterfly wings, eagle wings, dragonfly wings, crow wings. Rectangular and elliptical, feathered and smooth. The crisp orange-red of monarch butterflies, the soft downy white of pelicans.

"I have spent years trying to figure out what the wings mean," Max said. "Do the insects mean romantic heartbreak, the birds familial? The other way around? What discerns a butterfly from a crow?" Max shook their head. "I can't figure it out. The only thing I do know, is that those with wings can see Tranquility, and those without can't. I've asked Lilith why, but I don't think she knows either."

"How long have you been here?"

"Six years. I, like Josiah, stumbled across Tranquility while I was walking home. Came inside, met Robin first, actually. Ended up staying."

"Are you happy here?"

A warm, genuine, tight-lipped smile. "Oh, yes." Max's smile dimmed. "But I can tell that you wouldn't be, if you stayed," they said. "I think you know that, too."

Alice nodded. "I wouldn't be."

Max and Alice sat in the room, with the pinned butterflies on the walls, watching the wings through the window, in companionable silence, for the ensuing two hours. Customers drifted through the room, arriving in their suits and evening dresses, in suedes and silks and cottons.

Thursday. Raspberry oatmeal and scrambled eggs. *Practical Magic* by Alice Hoffman. Jeans and a purple sweatshirt, the same color purple as the irises on the table Alice had shared with Enid a couple nights ago.

Tranquility was open once more, but instead of taking up residence on the dining room couches, Alice was sitting on a stool beside Robin in the reception area. He had the thick tome of air fragrance records out on the desk and was recording customers and sales with a rose stamp dipped against a pad of blood-red ink. He placed their entrance fees in a cash box bespeckled with monarch butterfly stickers.

There was an influx of customers right around the dinner hour, but by the time eight o'clock rolled around, the reception area was quiet. "Okay!" Robin chirped, startling Alice out of *Practical Magic*. "Now!" Robin dramatically pulled up his sleeve to check his watch.

"Would you like to hear my Great Heartbreak? There's ample time before customers start departing."

Alice tucked her envelope-turned-bookmark into the pages of her book and set it on the counter, beside the now-closed tome. "I'd love to."

The butterflies on the walls stirred, a whispered hush beating between the unseen flap of their wings. "My Great Heartbreak is different from Josiah's and Lilith's. I don't see a romantic partner for my life, and I never have, so I don't have an Arnold or a Charles in my past. My Great Heartbreak is losing my sister, and my niece."

31

Tigard, Oregon, December 1973

Wren Vaughn was leaning against the porch railing of her parents' suburban home, a cigarette between her pointer and middle fingers, smoke curling in the early evening air. It was brisk, and she shivered in her thin, black, long-sleeved T-shirt and jeans. At her feet were two battered, brown suitcases, within which were all her worldly belongings. Shoved down her shirt, tucked into her bra, were her social security card, folded up birth certificate, $26, a debit card to an overdrawn checking account, and her drivers' license.

She was waiting.

Her parents were inside, oblivious that their daughter was standing on the porch, smoking. She didn't have to wait much longer. Her younger brother, Robin, would be home soon, and then everything would be okay.

Robin was a freshman at Portland State University. According to his latest call, his last final exam was that morning, and he would be back at their parents' house in time for dinner. Wren had attended PSU, too, a couple years ago. She dropped out after semester one and went to beauty school instead. She now worked at a beauty parlor in downtown Portland. Business wasn't booming, but it wasn't lackluster either. There was enough money to put food on the table and pay for her studio apartment.

Well. There *was*.

Wren waited only a couple minutes more until Robin's gray Pontiac LeMans pulled up the driveway. He cut the engine, stepped out of the car, and popped the trunk to grab his suitcase, wearing jeans and a sky-blue, vertical-striped button-down. He didn't see Wren. Not until he was clomping up the porch steps and swinging his keys around his pointer finger.

"Hey, Robin," Wren whispered, taking one last drag of her cigarette.

"Wren?" Robin dropped his suitcase on the porch with a heavy *thump* and tackled his sister in a tight bear hug. The paperwork tucked down Wren's shirt pressed against his chest, but he didn't notice. "It's so good to see you! What are you doing here?" He noticed the suitcases at Wren's feet. "Is everything okay?"

"No," Wren hiccupped. Robin tried to pull away from the hug to get a good look at his sister, but Wren tugged him tighter. "I'm pregnant, and out of a job," she said.

"Oh, Wren . . ." was all Robin said. He rubbed her back. "Do Mom and Dad know?"

"Not yet. I don't know how to tell them."

"We'll figure it out," Robin reassured. Because that was Robin. When they were in elementary school and Wren lost her jacket on the playground, Robin said, "We'll figure it out." When Wren's first boyfriend stood her up for prom her junior year and she couldn't find a date to take her, Robin said, "We'll figure it out," tugged on an oversized suit of their father's and took her. When Wren was in her first and only semester of college and realized that wasn't the path that was calling to her, Robin said, "We'll figure it out," and helped her research other career paths.

Her little brother always knew how to save her.

Mr. and Mrs. Vaughn took the news well, all things considered. Mrs. Vaughn turned a violent shade of purple for a couple of seconds, and Mr. Vaughn was two shallow breaths away from fainting, but by the end of the conversation, once Wren said that she used all of her savings on doctor's appointments and was missing work due to morning sickness and could no longer afford her apartment, her parents told her that she was welcome to stay in her childhood bedroom.

They didn't ask about the baby's father. Wren didn't say a word about who it was.

It was a couple days after Wren and Robin's arrival. It was a couple days before Christmas. Wren, Robin, and their mom were sitting around the kitchen table, which was covered with bottles of cylindrical sprinkles, undecorated sugar cookies shaped like gingerbread people and snowmen, and tubs of red, white, and green frosting with butterknife handles sticking out of them.

"Look, it's us!" Wren chirped, pointing at two gingerbread people whose hands had been baked together. "They're holding hands," she cooed.

The oven dinged in the kitchen, and their mom sprang to her feet, abandoning a half-decorated snowman to rescue the last tray of cookies before they burned—the last batch had been a bit too bronzed for her liking. Once she was out of earshot, Robin leaned toward Wren and asked, "Wren, what is the plan?"

"God, Robin, not right now." Wren rolled her eyes. "It's almost Christmas, for crying out loud."

"I leave in a week and a half, and I won't be back until summer break. You'll be . . . six or seven months along then? What are you going to do?"

Wren ran frosting fingers through her dark hair, leaving clumps of sugar and sprinkles in their wake. "Robin, I don't know what I'm going to do. I can't afford a baby. After the holidays, I'll go back to work, commute to downtown from here, save every penny that would have gone toward rent. Other than that, I don't know."

"Mom and Dad won't let you stay forever. I could take a gap year. Once I'm off for the summer, get a job, work full time, save up, we could get an apartment together."

"No!" Wren set down the hand-holding cookie she was decorating with red frosting and grabbed Robin by the shoulders. "I won't let you do that. You are getting educated. Don't let your screw-up older sister ruin that."

"Wren, you're not a screw-up."

Wren let go of Robin's shoulders and crossed her arms. "Yes, I am. I'm . . . pregnant off a one-night stand, barely twenty-two, can't pay my bills, living at home with my parents." She covered her mouth and sobbed into her hand. "And my little brother is offering to give up his education for me."

"I'm not giving anything up!" Robin grabbed Wren's shoulders this time. "And all of that *does not* make you a screw up! Not at all. It makes you human and going through a tough time."

Wren pulled Robin into a hug, each of them leaning awkwardly out of their chairs toward one another. "I'll figure out a plan," Wren promised. "Before you leave. One that does not involve you leaving school."

They hugged until their mom came back. "Everything alright?" she asked, arms laden with steaming hot undecorated cookies.

"Yes," Wren sniffled. She held up the hand-holding cookies again. "These are just making me nostalgic."

32

Tigard, Oregon, August 1974

Wren was in labor for sixteen hours before Linnet Vaughn was born, wailing and waving her arms as the nurses cleaned her. Robin and Mr. Vaughn were in the waiting room the whole time, taking turns pacing or feverishly napping. Waiting in the same trepid anticipation that Wren did, standing on that porch for Robin, eight months ago.

Mrs. Vaughn was with her daughter the whole time, holding her hand, fingers conjoined like the hand-in-hand gingerbread sugar cookie. She was there for the contractions and Wren's panicked pushing. She was there for the wailing of the baby. She was there when Wren cautiously ran a finger down her newborn's nose and murmured, "Linnet." She was there when Wren kept bleeding, and bleeding and bleeding, and bleeding still, until Wren's breathing stopped not long after Linnet's began.

And when Mrs. Vaughn rejoined her husband and son in the waiting room, she told them that they were going to raise a baby and that they needed to plan a funeral.

33

TIGARD, OREGON, SEPTEMBER 1974

Linnet was swaddled in Robin's arms, a tiny blue bundle of joy and spit-up. She was asleep, and Robin was staring down at her face, at her button nose and the crusties in the corners of her eyes. He was with Mrs. Vaughn in the kitchen as she prepped a bottle for when Linnet woke up screaming, which according to her routine, would be within the next thirty minutes.

Robin was leaving in two days to head back to school. He'd promised Wren before she went into labor that he wouldn't take any time off. As soon as he'd gone back for the winter quarter after Christmas and New Year's, he'd found a job at the public library restocking books and a job at a local pizza place as a cashier. Between both, he was working full-time, and he squirreled away every penny to help pay for diapers and onesies and whatever else the baby would need.

The old plan was to stay at their parents' house—they talked about that at length with their mom and dad—through the summer, until the baby came, and it was time for Robin to go back to school. Robin had found a cheap two-bedroom apartment close to campus, and Wren had found a beauty parlor nearby to work at. When Robin moved back to school, Wren and the baby would go with, and they would all live together.

But instead of spending his savings on rent and baby clothes, Robin helped his parents buy a casket for Wren. He insisted. The money was for her, anyway.

Robin couldn't cancel the lease on the apartment but found a buddy that was looking for a place. Mr. and Mrs. Vaughn were going to raise Linnet. In two days, Robin was going back to college, to that apartment destined for a different future, and not be able to come back home until Christmas. His insides writhed just thinking about it.

Linnet started stirring, squirming her little shoulders in her swaddle and clenching her eyes tighter as she prepared to wail. Mrs. Vaughn hurried over and handed Robin the bottle, and he eased the nipple of it into Linnet's mouth. Her eyes un-scrunched as she started eating.

"How much bigger do you think she'll get, while I'm gone?" Robin asked. His gray shirt smelled like baby spit-up, a curdled stench, but he might never smell like that again, after he moved back. Not from Linnet, at least.

"Don't think like that," Mrs. Vaughn admonished. She slung a dish towel over her shoulder and crossed her arms. "You'll see her grow up plenty." There were deep, purple bags under her eyes, and she watched Robin wearily.

Mr. Vaughn wasn't at retirement age yet, still working full-time, even more dedicated to getting a promotion now with a baby at home again. The Vaughns were okay financially, looking at a modest retirement for the two of them, but a baby, a newborn, with present and future expenses and a college fund, was putting stress on the future, especially because Mr. Vaughn had planned to retire right before Linnet would head off to college. Mrs. Vaughn wasn't a young mother, either. She'd thought her newborn days were far in the past.

"I could still stay back," Robin whispered. He rhythmically patted Linnet over her diaper butt with his hand.

"Robin, stop it!" Mrs. Vaughn flung her towel down on the kitchen counter with a snap. "You are going to school, and you're going to get a degree. That is what is top priority right now." Robin glanced down at Linnet in his arms.

The landline on the wall started ringing. Mrs. Vaughn glared at Robin for a solid three seconds before hurrying over to answer the phone. "Yes, this is she," she said into the receiver. "Oh . . . Oh . . . Um, okay." She hung the phone up in a daze, her hand holding the phone in place though there was no need to.

"Who was it?"

"That was a lawyer for some man that thinks he's Linnet's father. He wants a DNA test."

34

New York City, September 2009

Lilith Hubbard had gotten her heart broken. Again. Not Great Heartbreak territory or anything, but unpleasant, nonetheless. She'd really liked her.

Lilith was sitting at a bar a couple blocks over from Tranquility. It was a Tuesday evening, after Tranquility was quiet for the evening, and Lilith had an aversion to dishes. She'd knock back a couple gin and tonics here, then hurry back to Tranquility after that.

The bar was full, for a Tuesday night. The row of stools at the counter were nearly full, except for the one to Lilith's right. As the bartender slid her first gin and tonic of the night toward Lilith, a thin man hopped onto the seat and ordered a Manhattan. When the bartender gave the man his drink, Lilith stared longingly at the amber liquid, suddenly second-guessing her previous gin and tonic declaration.

"Are you alright, miss?" the man asked. He had dark hair, cropped close to his head on the sides but longer on top, and was wearing a navy-blue button down with black jeans.

"Oh, me?" Lilith asked. She switched her gaze from the man's drink to his face. There were laugh lines around his eyes, and Lilith figured he was in his early 50s. "Oh, I'll be alright. Heartbreak and all that." Lilith took a sip of her gin and tonic. "What about you, are you alright?"

"Oh, I'm sorry to hear that." The man hesitated before sharing his plight. "I'm coming off a ten-hour shift, but otherwise can't complain."

"Ten hours! Where do you work?"

"Restaurant a few blocks over. I'm a waiter."

"Ten hours is a long day," Lilith sighed, taking another sip. She side-eyed the man and pinched her lips together. "I'm a singer. Sometimes my workdays are ten hours too. But I enjoy it. Do you enjoy being a waiter?"

The man stared into his Manhattan and whispered, "I can pay my bills and live in New York City. That's enough." His voice was strained. "But a singer! Where do you sing?"

"Tranquility." Lilith swiveled in his seat, so that she was facing the man, waiting for his answer, leaning forward a millimeter more a second.

"Oh, that tiny club next to the drugstore, right? I've never been inside. Walked past it a couple times, though." He lifted his glass to his lips and poured half his drink down his throat. "I didn't know they were still in business. I've never seen an open sign."

"I own it."

"Pardon?"

"Tranquility. I'm the owner."

The man's eyes widened. "So, you're a business owner and a singer?"

"What's your name?"

The man guzzled the other half of his drink and waved the bartender over to order another. "Robin."

"Well, Robin, if you're in the market for another job, I'm hiring. Looking for a . . . receptionist of sorts. A Gatekeeper."

Robin shook his head and sighed. "Miss, you wouldn't want to hire me. I'm grateful for the job I have now, I don't think I could find another one."

"Why not?" Lilith was twirling a lock of her hair around her index finger with an elbow propped up on the counter.

Robin swallowed hard and clenched his jaw, opened and closed his mouth a few times before whispering, "Miss, I'm a convicted criminal. I'm awfully grateful for your offer, but my life is settled. If word got back to my manager that I was interviewing, I'd get fired. I can't lose my apartment." Robin's eyes were shifting back and forth, scanning the other bar patrons.

"Does your . . . criminality . . . have something to do with your Great Heartbreak?" Lilith was blatantly leaning forward in her chair now, her nose a mere six inches away from Robin's. He could discern the individual freckles on her cheeks and across the bridge of her nose.

"Miss, I'm not following."

Lilith leaned backward quickly and flushed. "I apologize, I can get . . . carried away." Lilith reached into her pocket and pulled out a business card. It was faint pink with a yellow chrysanthemum stamped in the corner, and the only thing written on it was her name and phone number. Lilith lowered her voice and said, "At Tranquility, I wouldn't be able to pay you much, but you'd have room and board in addition to your salary. There'd still be ten-hour days here and there. But I'd hope it would bring you more enjoyment than the job you have now. You could always stop by Tranquility sometime. It wouldn't be suspicious. It's a club!"

Robin quickly tucked the business card into the breast pocket of his button down. "Thank you," he said.

Lilith polished off the last of her gin and tonic and ordered another. Then Robin and Lilith sat side by side as they slowly savored their second drink each, until drifting out the door and parting, without speaking a word to one another.

Robin visited Tranquility the following evening. He stepped into the waiting room and was greeted with the aroma of sea salt and sugar cookies. It was as if he were at Canon Beach at age ten, swimming in the frigid ocean with Wren and ignoring their parents' calls to get out of the water or they'd catch a cold. The corners of his vision were fuzzy, and though he tried, he couldn't fully take in the room. He could see, however, a receptionist's desk lacking a receptionist and instead sporting a sign that read, "Welcome!" and had an arrow pointing to the right, to a red door.

Robin pulled open the door, wandered down a stout hallway, pushed aside gauzy pink curtains, and found himself in a dining room with a long bar and a stage. Robin sat at the bar and ordered a Manhattan, then watched the other patrons. They were even more dressed up than he was, unusual for him, in pantsuits and dresses, eating medium-rare steak or chicken parm or mac and cheese.

When Lilith had said Tranquility, Robin was picturing a run-down bar with sticky floors. This was not that.

And then, the velvet stage curtains parted, and onto the stage stepped Lilith, in a stunning silver gown with a plunging neckline down to her sternum and her strawberry blonde hair in long curls down her back. She pulled the microphone closer, like a lover leaning closer for a kiss, and began singing, "Can't Help Falling in Love." His heart began weeping. Vines grew from the ground, lithe and verdant and gentle, wrapping around the barstool legs and Robin's ankles, pinning him to the chair.

Robin put his head in his hands and waited for Lilith to spot him. To find him. To talk to him.

She did. Once her set finished, and the next singer stepped onstage, Lilith sat next to him at the bar and said, "Tell me."

So he did.

It was 1975. Robin was away at college, for his spring semester. Linnet's birth father took his parents to court and won. He got full custody. Robin didn't even get to say goodbye one last time. Linnet wasn't even one yet.

It was 1976. Linnet's birth father left her alone in her crib, in his two-bedroom, one-bath house on a record-breaking hot summer day. Linnet died. He swore he had a babysitter. Before it went to court, the story made local news. Robin saw it. Before it went to court, in the middle of the night, Robin poured a bottle of gasoline around the foundation of the father's house and tossed a match atop the wet line. He watched flames engulf the house, a physical manifestation of what losing Wren and Linnet had done to his heart.

It was 1994. Robin was let out of prison early on good behavior, a hollowed-out man, a man with an unfinished education, a man his parents had disowned, a man his deceased sister would be ashamed of, a man who had nothing but himself. He moved to New York City. Lost himself in the crowd of millions. Became numb.

"I think Wren would have loved it here," Robin sniffled, wiping his snotty nose on his sleeves. "Are you still hiring?"

Lilith draped an arm around Robin's shoulders and leaned her head against his. The vines that entangled Robin retreated into the ground. "Yes."

35

New York City, March 2022

Robin cried as he concluded his story, wiping tears away with a navy-blue pocket square he'd pulled from thin air. Alice was teary-eyed, too.

"I've been here ever since!" Robin proclaimed. "I lived here for a couple years, until deciding that living on my own would be for the best. I wanted a cat and Lilith is allergic. If I'd finished college, my degree would have been in accounting, and before I got here, I don't know how Lilith kept afloat. I take care of the finances. Lilith calls me the Gatekeeper. I'm the bridge between the material world and Tranquility."

Robin cleared his throat and motioned to *Practical Magic* with a wave of his hand. "Now, customers will be on their way out soon, and you have reading to do."

"Thank you, Robin," Alice murmured. "For sharing. And for the books."

"No, thank *you* Alice. Being a good listener is one of the best things a person can be. And how'd you know the books were me?"

Alice picked up *Practical Magic* and pointed to the first page, where Lilith had written, "To my Robin," with a caricature of a bird—presumably a robin—except Lilith was not artistically inclined and it was more of a blob with a beak.

"I'm not known for my stealth," Robin laughed. The butterflies in the walls strained against their pins, reaching as close to Robin as they could.

Friday morning. Blueberry pancakes and scrambled eggs. *I Capture the Castle* by Dodie Smith. This morning, instead of eating alone in her room, Alice took the breakfast tray out to the dining room.

The stage was dark, the tables empty, except laughter floated out of the kitchen. Alice padded past the bar and into the kitchen, which was a rectangular space with a wide stove, industrial oven and refrigerator, a butcher block island, and doorless cabinets. Lilith was picking blueberries out of a clear bowl of dwindling pancake batter and popping them in her mouth, batter coating and all, while Mateo wasn't looking.

"Oh, good morning!" Lilith said, noticing Alice with her breakfast tray.

"Can I join you?"

"Of course," Mateo said as he flipped two pancakes onto a plate for Lilith. "I am heading out as soon as the batter runs out, though. It's career day at my daughter's school."

There were no chairs in the kitchen, so Lilith and Alice stood around the island. Lilith drowned her pancakes in butter and syrup. Alice ate her pancakes in dainty little pre-cut bites. Mateo hummed while he flipped the rest of the pancakes.

"Thank you for breakfast this week," Alice said as Mateo turned off the stove.

"You're welcome," Mateo replied with a wink. He let the kitchen doors swing closed behind him.

Alice turned to look at Lilith and said, all at once, in a rush, forcing herself to say it before she could stop herself, "Aunt Lilith, thank you for letting me stay this week, and I know you invited me to stay through Sunday, but I think I should leave tonight."

Lilith didn't react, neither positively nor negatively. She simply said, "What is your reasoning?"

"I'm grateful to all the people I've met, but I need a few days by myself, before break ends, to straighten up my dorm. Get organized." Alice glanced down at her empty pancake plate, then back up at Lilith. "I have a life to live, and I think it's time to go live it."

A genuine smile slowly crept across Lilith's face. "Don't buffer your words with an 'I think!' You're right, and I'm proud of you."

Alice laughed, a half-relieved, half-happy laugh that erupted as she sighed. "Besides, I still have an English lit essay to write, too."

"Robin can walk you back to your dorm after dinner tonight. But before you go, there's one more Great Heartbreak you need to hear."

Alice ran through who was left to talk to. Lilith, Mateo, Vincent, Carmela, Josiah, Enid, Robin. It couldn't be Max. "Whose?"

Lilith fiddled with the ends of her hair and sighed, "Mine."

36

SEATTLE, WASHINGTON, NOVEMBER 1999

Ellie was curled into herself in her bed, with its cream, percale linens and amber duvet discarded on the floor. Ellie's thinning hair fell like a shroud around her shoulders. Her eyes were permanently puffy, crusted salt residue was matted into the hair at her temples, and her under-eyes were rubbed raw from repeatedly wiping away tears with tissues.

Beside the bed was an empty bassinet, shrouded in frilly pink lace.

Lilith stood in the doorway, half her body angled into the bedroom and the other half lingering in the hallway. Her suitcase was in the front entryway. She'd just been dropped off by a cab from the airport, and when Ellie wasn't answering her calls, Lilith found a spare key under the black and white striped welcome mat and let herself in. "Hi, Els," Lilith whispered.

Ellie rotated in the bed, like an armadillo unfurling, to take in Lilith standing there, hovering. "What are you doing here, Lils?" she croaked.

"Is James here?" Lilith asked.

"He's staying with his parents this weekend," Ellie squeaked. She pushed aside the thin sheet draped across her and sat up, swinging her feet off the bed, facing Lilith. Beneath her shirt, Lilith could tell that Ellie's stomach was still rounded.

"Do you want me to call James—"

"No!" Ellie stared at the ground. "I'm fine."

Lilith took hesitant steps toward the bed. She was not invited here, this she knew. There was no emphatic phone call between them, just a clipped phone call from their mother. "Ellie needs you," their mother had said. "She won't let me help her, but she might let you." That was all it took for Lilith to shove bulky thrifted sweaters and a toothbrush into a bag, book an overpriced airline ticket, and risk the wrath of her girlfriend, Juniper, as Lilith left her behind on their anniversary weekend.

Ellie stared at her feet, scrubbed a hand down her face, kneaded an eye with her forefinger.

Lilith asked, "Can I cook you any—"

Ellie's head whipped upward, and she glared at her sister. "I didn't ask you to come here! I know Mom probably asked you to babysit me, but I don't need you here. I don't need Mom here. I don't need James here."

"When was the last time you've eaten?"

"Lils, you cannot understand what I'm going through."

"When was the last time you ate?"

Ellie shuffled off the bed, her feet landing on the cream carpet with a *thump*. She waddled closer to Lilith, and Lilith stood her ground. "I don't need you here." Ellie spit. "All you're going to do is stare at me in pity while you're thinking about how it's not so bad if you never have kids. You don't need kids to be happy and all that bullshit. You will never understand what it is like to hold your lifeless newborn in your arms. You and your child-free pretentiousness." Ellie was snarling now, the bags under her eyes growing deeper.

"Els," Lilith managed to whisper, "I am here as your sister, who loves you, to support you. I do not have to want to be a mother to do that. I am here for you as you need."

"I need you to go away!"

Lilith squared her shoulders and let the fraught silence hang. "Fine." She shook her head and bunched up her lips. "I know you're hurting, more than you ever have in your life, but that does not give you the right to yell at me for having different life goals. What we want our lives to look like is neither here nor there right now."

"Get out." Ellie stared at the ground. She didn't glance up as Lilith disappeared down the hallway, took her suitcase, and left, making sure to lock the door and put the spare key back under the doormat where she'd found it. If her sister didn't want her, *fine*. There was still time to make it back to she and Juniper's Los Angeles apartment and celebrate their three years together.

Lilith nearly dropped her keys as she juggled the handle of her suitcase, a bouquet of multicolored chrysanthemums, an elephant—Juniper's favorite animal—plush, and a mantra of apologies for missing their anniversary. It was just after midnight, and Lilith's determination to find fresh flowers this late at night was the reason she'd missed their official anniversary day by mere minutes.

The black-painted apartment door clicked open, and Lilith shoved it aside to haul in her accoutrements. "June-bug," Lilith began humming, abandoning all but the flowers and the plush just over the threshold. "June-bug, I'm—"

Lilith and Juniper shared a studio apartment. No walls between entryway, kitchen, living room, bedroom. A singular view. There was Lilith's June-bug, cradled around another woman in the plush bed, their bare limbs intertwined, their hair knotted together, their noses nuzzling, even in sleep. They were curled up like cats.

Lilith caged a scream between her teeth. She threw the elephant plush at the sleeping women, startling Juniper awake, but Lilith couldn't pry the bouquet of flowers from her clenched fist.

"Who's there!" Juniper cried out, and Lilith ignored her, instead crossing the apartment in broad strides, crouching down, and rifling through her nightstand. Lilith grabbed her social security card, her birth certificate, and her previous years' tax filings, and carried them to the entryway. "Who is it?

Lilith still didn't respond. She slammed the bouquet down on the floor, tilted her suitcase over like a demolished silo, and unzipped it, then began shoving her documents on top of her clothes. There was a hand on Lilith's shoulder, and there was Juniper, wrapped haphazardly in a creamy-white bedsheet. "Lily, I'm so sorry!" she wailed. Lilith shook off Juniper's hand, but Juniper bent down beside Lilith, picking up the flowers and cradling them against her chest. She pinched the petals between her fingers, bruising them. "Are these for me? Lily—it's not what you think! It doesn't mean anything, you're my world—"

"Do not speak to me," Lilith said, monotone. She started zipping up her suitcase, but Juniper slammed the bouquet atop it in a spray of petals and pollen, then held her palms flat, crushing the flowers further.

"Lily, don't leave," she squeaked.

Lilith stilled, as did Juniper. Lilith let go of the suitcase, cradled Juniper's head in her hands, and Juniper's hands gently clasped Lilith's wrists. Lilith brushed Juniper's tears away with her thumbs and whispered, "I thought I knew what a Great Heartbreak was, before you. But apparently, I knew *nothing*."

Before Juniper could stop her, Lilith zipped up her suitcase, bouquet and all, and she left, the apartment door slamming closed behind her. Juniper's lover was still asleep in bed.

Lilith bought a one-way ticket to New York City. As soon as her flight landed, she called a real estate agent to inquire about commercial property available for sale. Lilith bought Tranquility and drained every last penny from her and Juniper's shared account.

When Lilith was unpacking in her new home, she still had the chrysanthemums Juniper had shoved in the suitcase. Lilith couldn't throw them away, but instead wrapped them in a mud-brown turtleneck that Juniper had gifted as a birthday present and let them suffocate in the bottom of her suitcase.

Standing in her bedroom at Tranquility, Lilith stared at the wilting petals, at the mottled creases Juniper left with her fingers, the patches of missing petals, the squished stems. With teary eyes and a huff, Lilith marched out of the bedroom and hurled the sweater-wrapped bouquet against the floor.

Lilith returned a few hours later, prepared to toss the flowers in the trash, but at her feet was only the sweater, its arms splayed out awaiting an embrace. The wilting blooms had already migrated to the walls.

37

New York City, March 2022

Alice sat on the edge of her bed, her phone in her hands. She did not struggle against the vines that began growing from the carpet. She didn't call out for Harold.

Alice raised her phone to her ear and listened to the dial tone, then her mother's voice saying, "Hi, sweets, how are you?"

"Can I talk to you now? About Rylan?" Alice asked. She fisted the bedsheets around her free hand and watched as the vines crawled up to her shins.

"Of course."

"Rylan told me that if he married me, he'd want to have an affair," Alice blurted. "The night we broke up. He said he'd want to have an affair if he stayed with me."

The line was quiet, the vines kept climbing, until Ellie whispered, "Your father and I nearly divorced, and yet he has never once been unfaithful to me. *Ever*. The thought hasn't even crossed his mind, and same for me. That boy did not love you as you deserve. Not even close."

“Not even close,” Alice repeated.

“Not even close,” her mother echoed.

Alice stared at her ankles. Reached down. Caressed the vice-like vines until they sluffed away like an ebbing ocean tide.

And the Crimson-Black and Pink Dahlias

5

38

New York City, March 2022

Alice's time at Tranquility ended Friday evening. She packed up her belongings, deciding to wear the lingerie she'd been afraid of beneath a bulky sweater and distressed jeans.

Robin walked Alice back to her dorm building, once again refusing to let her carry her own bag. Outside the building, Robin gave Alice a hug and told her to come visit after her next Great Heartbreak. She thanked him for the books and said that she'd left them on her nightstand. Robin handed her a weathered copy of *The Virgin Suicides* by Jeffrey Eugenides to keep and said that it had been her mother's.

Alice couldn't wait to tell Devi about the week she'd had, just as she was sure that Devi was bursting at the seams to tell Alice about Spain. Alice knew, however, that she wasn't going to tell Devi about the Great Heartbreaks of the people she'd met, or anyone else. They weren't her stories to tell.

Back in her dorm, Alice stripped the light blue sheets off her bed and washed them. She straightened up her desk, throwing away the letters from Rylan with its peculiar pollen puddle. Her chest still ached, but not as much as before.

Alice unzipped her suitcase. Resting on top of her clothes was a bouquet of mildly crushed orange daffodils, white daisies, and bluebells wrapped in cellophane. They were fragrant, smelling of the lavender, vanilla, and balsam of Tranquility. Alice brought the flowers to her nose and breathed in.

Knowing

Savannah, Georgia, March 2000

Mateo Cruz wiped his palms on the cloth restaurant napkin for the fifth time and checked his watch face, noting that the hands hadn't ticked much farther than the last time he checked. Felix wasn't usually late. And he wouldn't be late to this.

Felix and Mateo had been together for a year and a half, as of a few days ago. They hadn't had the chance to celebrate—Mateo was an entry-level tax accountant, and it was busy season, and Felix had been out of town on a business trip—but their schedules aligned on a Saturday evening in a warm spring. Mateo's underarms were damp from the heat, and he hoped sweat stains weren't blooming on his navy-blue button down.

Mateo took another sip from his half-full glass of water, the condensation from the glass adding to the slickness of his sweaty palms. Buried in his pants pocket was a box, and within the box was a key to his apartment. Mateo was going to ask Felix to move in with him.

It was a big step, but it was a step that felt *right*. Mateo had never felt so content in a relationship before. He and Felix both had a love of travel and cared about their families, and one day wanted a family together. They liked the same movies, had the same taste in music, and wholeheartedly believed that music on a record player had a quality modern technology could never replicate. Shared passionate goals abounded. Plus, Felix was the hottest man Mateo had ever seen, with crisp blue eyes, curly black hair, and one of those waists that tapers inward like a fairy-tale prince.

It wasn't like Felix to be late, especially not to a semi-anniversary dinner. The waiter stopped by to refill Mateo's water glass, and Mateo glanced back down at his watch. Surely, Felix would be there soon.

They'd picked an upscale Italian restaurant for the evening. The lighting was dimmed, and pink candles flickered on the tabletops. Mateo was sitting at a booth in the corner of the room, and on the walls were framed black-and-white pictures of the founder, the founder's family, and various celebrities that had stopped by the establishment over the years. Interspersed were shelves with fake fruits and vegetables resting atop them, their plastic coated in dust.

Mateo had gone for another sip of his drink just as Felix arrived. Felix hurried through the restaurant, nearly colliding with a waiter holding a tray full of saucy pastas but managing to skirt around him with whispered apologies. He slid into the booth across from Mateo.

"So sorry," Felix said, rolling up the sleeves of his white-and-green-striped button down. "It's been a long day."

"No, no," Mateo replied. "It's okay, I understand." He set his water glass back down on the table.

"Give me a sec to look over the menu, and we'll order as soon as the waiter gets here," Felix said, lifting his laminated menu and pressing his nose close to the pages. He needed reading glasses, desperately, but refused to wear them on principle. They made his nose greasy, and he hated how he looked in glasses. Mateo didn't agree, but such things were not left up to him.

The two men sat in silence while Felix scanned the menu, and when the waiter walked over in the next few minutes, they both ordered—Mateo the Bolognese and Felix the carbonara. Felix took a few more moments to sip on his water glass while Mateo simmered in his own anxious sweat, the apartment key heavy in his pocket.

"This day has been exhausting," Felix sighed, leaning back in the booth. The ambient sounds of silverware and hushed conversations burbled up around them. "And I'm so sorry I'm late. There was a work emergency."

"It's okay, love, I understand." Mateo wiped his palms on his napkin again—the sixth time this evening—and cleared his throat. "There's actually something I would like to discuss.

"Oh?" Felix's brow creased. "Is everything okay?"

"Yes! Yes, nothing . . . it's just something that's been on my mind lately."

"Okay . . ." Felix unfolded his napkin-wrapped silverware and set the cloth napkin on his lap, then he started reaching for Mateo's hand across the table. "What's on your mind, babe?"

"I—" The waiter chose that moment to deliver a basket of fresh-baked bread, two small, pre-cut loaves with crispy crusts and a cup of garlic butter. Felix pulled his hand back, and Mateo stared at the bread as Felix buttered up a slice for himself. "I've been thinking lately."

"Yes?" Felix was preoccupied with his bread, pinching the crusts between his fingers. Mateo was simmering in his ineloquence; he'd rehearsed this speech in the bathroom mirror for an hour this morning, and already he was butchering it. He couldn't even get the words out.

"I want you to move in with me," Mateo blurted. Felix stopped chewing as Mateo pulled the box out of his pocket and opened it. The apartment key had a red bow, tied crookedly, around it, and the metal glinted in the flame from the candle on the table.

"Mateo . . ." Felix said. He swallowed his bite of bread, grimacing as it went down. His gaze darted around their table and he tugged on the collar of his shirt. "*Wow*, that's a . . . big step."

"I know it is. I know." Mateo took a deep breath and laced his fingers together. "But I've been thinking about this a lot, and I am ready to take this step with you. I see a future with you, and with how busy our schedules are, I think we would be better able to spend time with one another if we lived in the same place." Mateo grabbed Felix's hand across the table. "This would be a decision both out of practicality and love."

"Oh, Mateo," Felix said. He had gone pale, and his lips were pinched together. "Can I think about it?" Felix pushed the box with the key in it back across the table.

"Yeah." Mateo, with shaking hands, grabbed the box and shoved it back into his pocket, quickly. "Yeah, of course. Take all the time you need." Mateo reached for a slice of the bread and slathered the garlic butter on it, his face flushed.

Felix and Mateo were silent as they nibbled on the bread, already slightly stale and cold. They avoided eye contact as the Bolognese and carbonara arrived.

When the meal had nearly concluded, Felix said, "I don't think moving in together would be such a great idea." His head was bowed, his voice directed toward his half-eaten plate.

"Why not?" Mateo asked, setting down his fork and wiping his mouth with his helplessly damp napkin.

"I think it's too soon."

"Okay. So, what time are you thinking then? A year from now? Two?"

"Why don't we just take things as they come?"

Mateo pressed his lips together and he folded his hands in his lap, also staring down at his half-eaten food, unable to meet Felix's eyes. "I guess I misunderstood where we were at in our relationship."

"No—Mateo, that's not it—"

"Then what is it?" Mateo looked up at Felix, to find him helplessly pale and holding back tears.

"It didn't mean anything. I swear."

Mateo's stomach turned, the Bolognese doing somersaults. "*What* didn't mean anything?" Felix turned his head to the side, staring out into the restaurant and the other diners happily swirling pastas around their forks. "Talk to me."

"Lucia's pregnant."

Mateo blinked a few times. "She is? How do you know that? What does that have to do with us?"

"No." Felix put his elbows on the table and hid his face in his hands. "Lucia's pregnant, and the baby's . . . the baby is . . ."

Mateo's heart sank. He processed the words slowly, trying to make sense of them, then he was trembling, head to toe, torn between crying and seething. "You knocked up *my sister?*"

"It was an accident! It didn't mean *anything*. We were both drunk, and I—"

Mateo stood up and flung his napkin down on the table, his head spinning. "There are no words to describe how disgusting you are."

"Mateo! Wait—" Felix called, trying to follow him out of the restaurant, but the waiter intercepted, asking for a payment method. Mateo's eyes burned, his heart numb, unable to process the betrayal as he walked back to his apartment, alone.

Savannah, Georgia
May 2000

The homes of the historic district shone in the fading sunlight, and Mateo kept his head down against the glare as he walked back to his apartment after work. He'd taken the long way. The excessively long way, looping through the historic district and wandering through Forsyth Park, squares, cemeteries, meandering his way back home. It had been a hard two months.

When Mateo got home after his dinner with Felix, he called Lucia and asked her for the truth. Mateo hadn't spoken to Lucia or Felix since. He'd blocked both their numbers, and when his mother tried to intervene—especially on behalf of Lucia because blood is thicker than water—Mateo had said simply, softly, dejectedly, "Mamá, no puedo hablar con estos traidores. No les debo nada. Especialmente Lucia." She'd dropped the issue, and Mateo refused to even entertain the idea of a family gathering if Lucia would be in attendance. Lucia and Felix were both dead to him.

Initially, Mateo had thrown himself into his work. But tax season was over now, and Mateo struggled to fill the hours. He'd taken to wandering the city, up and down the streets, lingering in the shadows of homes over a century old, reading about the ghosts of the city, and wondering if he was one of those ghosts the tourists came to gawk at.

On this particular May evening, Mateo was approaching his apartment building after walking the entire length of Oglethorpe Avenue twice. The underarms of his gray dress shirt were damp with sweat from the warm evening, and he was still carrying his leather work briefcase. As Mateo stepped toward the door to the apartment building, he stopped suddenly.

Felix was standing outside the door.

"Mateo, can I talk to you for a second?" Felix asked. Mateo stood there blinking for a few seconds, taking in Felix's scruffy hair, the circles under his blue eyes, and his unshaved cheeks.

"No." Mateo turned on his heel and started walking away, but Felix jogged and caught up.

"Mateo, I'm really sorry. I need to tell you something."

The two men, in step with one another, were walking at a brisk pace back the way Mateo came. "Then speak."

"The baby's not mine."

Mateo steeled his features into a monotone mask. "So what?"

"So!" Felix grabbed Mateo by the shoulders, pulling them up short in the middle of the sidewalk beneath a streetlight. "Lucia lied to me. I'm not the father. I am so sorry for . . . for everything. You are everything I've ever wanted, and I will spend the rest of my life begging for forgiveness if you would please give me another chance."

Mateo stared at Felix, both of their chests heaving up and down as if they'd just swum the English Channel. "You still cheated on me."

"Well, yes, but—"

"But nothing. You cheated on me. With my *sister*."

"It didn't mean anything. It was an accident, and—"

"I am having a very difficult time understanding how cheating on me with my sister multiple times was an accident." Felix grew pale and sweat shone on his forehead. "Yea, Lucia did tell me that much."

Felix's fingers pressed into Mateo's shoulders, and he leaned their foreheads together. He lowered his voice and tears beaded along his lash line. "Losing you would be the greatest mistake of my entire life. I love you, Mateo. I always have and I always will, and I can't live the rest of my life without you. I want to travel the world with you. I want a family with you. Please, Mateo. Give me another chance."

Mateo kept their foreheads pressed together and let Felix talk, silently mulling over the words that passed between them. He desperately wanted to say *Let's go back to mine. Bygones. You're my forever*. This was the man he'd envisioned spending his life with. People made mistakes, didn't they? Mateo could forgive. Because how could he give up on their once-in-a-lifetime love story? Meeting in Madison Square on a bright autumn afternoon, both new to the city after recent college graduations, then stumbling into a nearby chocolatier together, swapping secrets and chocolates for hours. They could be as they were before. Blissful.

But how could Mateo justify taking Felix back? How would anyone be convinced that it was a healthy choice, anyone but himself?

"Felix," Mateo whispered, his chest aching as he pulled away. "How could I live, knowing what you mean to me and that I didn't mean the same to you? How could I live, knowing the example you would set for our children?"

"No, Mateo—"

"How could I live, knowing that taking you back is the wrong choice?"

Felix's mouth gaped open and close, a fish out of water, and he whispered, "I miss you. I love you."

"Those are just words." Mateo stared into Felix's eyes, took a deep breath, and said to the man he'd thought was the love of his life, "I never want to see you again." With that, Mateo turned around and walked away.

Jump

Black River Falls, Wisconsin
July 2011

Jenifer Brooks sat in her gold Toyota Camry at the far end of the hospital parking lot, her forehead pressed against the leather steering wheel, tears falling straight from her swollen eyelids to her lap. Her hands were wrapped around the wheel, to either side of her head, fingertips white and palms slick with sweat. Tate didn't mean it. Surely, he didn't mean it. He wasn't thinking clearly through all the drugs dripping from the IV into his bloodstream. They would get through this.

"Jen?" Billy's voice crackled over the car speakers. "Jen, talk to me."

Jenifer sniffled, leaning back in her seat. She reached over and popped open the glove box, rifling past 2000s Black Eyed Peas, P!nk, and Carrie Underwood CDs to grab a fistful of spare Dunkin' Donuts napkins to mop up her splotchy face.

"Jen—"

"I should go back in there," Jen said. Her voice was low and gravelly. "He didn't mean it, I should—"

"Jen, go home. Tate doesn't want you there."

"No, I—"

"Jen!" Billy's voice grew louder over the phone, and Jenifer assumed he had the receiver pressed up against his lips. "It's a shitty thing that happened. And it's even shittier how Tate's reacting. But he's a grown ass man and right now there's nothing you can do." Billy's breath crinkled across the connection. "Okay?"

"Okay." Jenifer was back to pressing her forehead against the steering wheel, watching her teardrops make dark, wet ovals on her light-wash jeans.

"I think you should come out and visit me."

Jenifer let the silence hang as she tapped tear-saturated napkins to her lash line. "I can't just—"

"I'm buying you a plane ticket. You need to get out of that goddamn town. Mom and Dad will understand, I'll call them and let them know what's going on. How long do you need to pack?"

"You don't have to—"

"I do. You need a few days away from it all."

Jenifer stared out her windshield, squinting at the squat hospital building, at the maroon and white banners hanging from awnings and light posts. "Book it out of Minneapolis. You might be able to find a direct flight."

New York City
July 2011

Jenifer flew into LaGuardia that afternoon. Billy was waiting for her just beyond security and baggage claim, wearing dark wash jeans and a flannel in eighty-degree weather. He took her suitcase from her—a pink-shelled carry-on, Jenifer's half of a matching set she shared with Tate—and ushered her into a taxi, off to find his Manhattan apartment. They slid into the backseat. Jenifer leaned her head against Billy's shoulder, watching pedestrians and the New York cityscape pass by through the window as their taxi meandered through the city.

Billy lived in a studio apartment on the third floor of a fifty-story Manhattan skyscraper. Instead of waiting for the elevator, they took the stairs, Billy carrying Jenifer's luggage up for her. When they reached Billy's apartment and Billy pushed open the door, he said, "Make yourself comfortable." He set Jenifer's carry-on at the foot of the bed and poured Jenifer a glass of orange juice, their childhood comfort drink. Their mom used to handmake orange juice, squeezing pulpy oranges into a glass jug on warm summer afternoons. Billy's orange juice was store bought, but it would do.

"Thanks, Billy," Jenifer said, giving him a hug, her head resting against his chest. She was short, compared to Billy's tall. Jenifer had taken after their dad's side of the family, barely clearing five feet and perpetually struggling to find pants that fit her. Billy took after their mom's side, seeming to grow into the stratosphere.

"So I was thinking," Billy began as Jenifer sipped on the orange juice.

"That sounds dangerous," Jenifer replied with a raised eyebrow. Her eyes were still puffy, and she hadn't risked wearing makeup since Tate's accident. She'd just cry the mascara off, giving herself permanent racoon eyes.

"I think we should go out tonight."

"Bills," Jenifer sighed, setting the empty glass on his laminate kitchen counter with a *clink*. "I'm really not in the mood."

"You're not in the mood for anything right now except moping about."

"Do you blame—blame me?" Jenifer hiccupped, more tears welling behind her eyes as her breath hitched.

"No—wait—that's not—" Billy stammered, pulling Jenifer into a hug. "I just think that we could go out for dinner or something. Not just sit around here, with you waiting for Tate to call." Billy lowered his voice. "And he's not going to."

"I...Okay," Jenifer sighed, her stomach rumbling. She could go for a good wood-fired pizza, or a medium rare steak, or a juicy burger, or a glass of wine. "I'll get changed."

Jenifer and Billy were strolling through the Manhattan streets, bellies full of greasy hamburgers, crunchy fries, and cheap beer. Billy was still wearing his jeans and flannel, but Jenifer had changed into a flouncy white dress with halter straps and a layered skirt.

They were at a street corner, waiting to cross, when the scent of saltwater taffy wafted toward them. Jenifer put her hand on Billy's shoulder and said, "Do you smell that?"

Billy stuck his nose in the air, nostrils flaring. "I don't smell anything besides city stink."

Jenifer stepped away from the street corner, walking backwards, her nose turned upwards. "The saltwater taffy from that trip with Mom and Dad to the beach when we were kids? You don't smell it?"

"You have a nose like a hound."

Jenifer turned around, facing the stores they just passed. She stared at a dark alley directly behind them, then at a luminescent drugstore, its windows buzzing with blinking lights. Smooshed between the two was a door with a painted sign above it, on which the word "Tranquility" was written in white cursive. Jenifer stood in front of the door, crimson-red painted with a metal toad sculpture for a handle.

Jenifer didn't look back at Billy. She reached out and pulled open the door. Beyond it was a small reception area, with a long spruce wood desk and flooring made of white tiles with blue grout. The smell of saltwater taffy permeated the room, while Billy, who had followed Jenifer in, kept rubbing his nose.

"Hello. How can I help you?" Jenifer and Billy blinked a few times, hearing before seeing, until suddenly there was a man standing behind the reception desk.

"Hello," Jenifer said. "What is this place?"

"Welcome to Tranquility," the man said. He was dressed in a plum-colored wool suit and wore wiry spectacles low on his nose. "Let's get you signed in."

Jenifer and Billy were sitting at a circular table in a dimly lit dining room, watching a woman with strawberry blonde hair wearing a floor-length gossamer gown sing love ballads to a crowd of people dressed in anything from suits and dresses to sweatpants and athleisure. The patrons sipped on martinis and swayed in their seats along with the music, Jenifer silently weeping all the while. Billy kept shooting his sister sidelong glances as she sniffled and used the flounces of her skirt as tissues.

After a fifth performance, the woman stepped off the stage and into the crowd, accepting white lilies and red roses from the other patrons, the midnight blue skirt of her gown trailing after her like a receding ocean wave. The woman reached Jenifer and Billy's table, and instead of continuing on her way, she pulled out a chair beside Jenifer and sat down.

"I'm Lilith," the woman murmured, reaching out and taking Jenifer's hand while cradling the bouquet of flowers in the crook of her opposite arm. Jenifer stared at Lilith with wide eyes, and Billy glanced back and forth between the two women. "Are you alright, dear?"

"Oh," Jenifer said, wiping at her cheeks with the palm of her free hand. "Oh, I'm fine. I just—it's been—it's been a hard week."

"I am here to listen, if you need an ear," Lilith hummed. She plucked one of the lilies from her bouquet and offered it to Jenifer, the petals curling back in elegant swirls. Lilith stood up, continuing on her way through the room, her dress floating behind her.

"Jen, we should head home," Billy said, resting his palm against Jenifer's shoulder.

The two siblings stumbled out onto the Manhattan streets, meandering their way back to Billy's apartment. Jenifer hugged herself, her hands wrapped around her elbows.

"Billy?" Jenifer whispered as they puffed their way up the apartment building stairs. "I have to go back and talk to that woman. To Lilith."

Billy opened and closed his mouth a few times, a fish gaping out of water. "Okay," was all he said as he unlocked his apartment door.

"What is it that you'd like to talk about, dear?" Lilith asked.

Jenifer and Lilith were sitting backstage on a plush, orange-leather couch. Lilith was wearing a gray ball gown, and a bouquet of blue and purple hyacinths were lying on a vanity table nearby. The lights were dim. Jenifer had sought out Lilith after the show. The two women had ducked behind the curtain, maneuvered their way through a maze of vanities to the couch, and sunk into the leather.

"What is this place?" Jenifer asked. She threaded her fingers together and whispered, "That's not all I'd like to say, but I just . . . wanted to ask. Again. I didn't really get an answer before, from the receptionist."

"Hmm," Lilith hummed, "Tranquility is a place founded from heartache."

Jenifer waited for Lilith to say more, but when she didn't, Jenifer said softly, "I'm going through heartache."

"I am here to listen," Lilith replied, offering Jenifer a patient smile.

Jenifer bit her lip—silently telling herself that this was *crazy*, talking to some off-her-rocker woman at a dingy nightclub—and said, "Tate and I are—were—high school sweethearts. He told me . . . he promised that he would marry me on our fifth anniversary. This past weekend, I thought—I thought he was going to propose." Jenifer's forehead scrunched, and she put her head in her hands."Start at the beginning," Lilith said. "Start at the beginning and tell it slowly, one puzzle piece at a time."

Jenifer took a deep breath.

Lake Wazee, Wisconsin
July 2011

Tate and Jenifer stood at the top of the cliff, a breeze tugging at their hair and wrapping around their sunbaked skin. Jenifer tilted her face upwards, into the late afternoon sunshine, letting the warmth soak into her bare shoulders and stomach and legs, all the skin exposed by her black bikini. Tate had his arm around Jenifer's waist, his hand pressed to her bare side, fingers spread out.

"Are you going to jump with me?" Tate asked. Jenifer turned away from the sun toward Tate, taking note of his bright blue eyes and the freckles smattered across his nose and bare chest. She'd tried to count them, once, a few years ago, as they'd laid in his Purdue dorm room bed on a lazy Saturday in October.

"Jen?" Tate asked again. "Jump with me?"

"In a minute," Jenifer replied, looking down at the glistening lake below them. "It's gorgeous from up here."

"Mmmhmm."

It was their fourth anniversary, in a few days.

They'd grown up together, attending St. Joseph Catholic Church since they were babies, struggling through algebra and chemistry classes in middle school and high school, knowing of one another for over a decade before Tate asked Jenifer to the prom their junior year. "You want to go with me?" Tate had asked Jenifer at the homecoming football game, during halftime. He'd walked right off the field, straight to the stands, to where Jenifer was standing atop the bleachers wrapped in a blanket with her best friend.

"What?" Jenifer had laughed, and her friend tugged on her arm.

"Go to the prom with me." Tate's jersey was askew, the orange "12" grass-stained, and his cheeks were smudged in black chalk. His sweaty blond hair was sticking up in odd directions, like duck tails.

"Okay."

"I'll pick you up at seven."

Tate and Jenifer had been inseparable ever since. The lovebirds. The high school sweethearts. Their Instagram pages were plastered with formal dances and graduation and travel. Jenifer went to beauty school, Tate off to Purdue to study mechanical engineering. Now, Tate was starting his senior year in the fall. They'd been together for so long already. Jenifer was waiting for him to ask her to marry him.

She thought he might propose at Lake Wazee. Tate was home for the summer, working as a technician at Grassland Dairy on the weekdays, and outside exploring with Jenifer on the weekends. They hiked and swam and camped. But this was their last free day before their anniversary. Surely, he had something up his sleeve, like a photographer in the woods or a glittery engagement ring.

"Everything alright?" Tate asked, squeezing Jenifer on the shoulder.

"Just thinking," Jenifer replied.

"Okay. Ready to jump?"

"On three."

They took a few steps backward, then dashed to the cliff's edge, jumping at the same time, plummeting down twenty-five feet, whooping all the while. Jenifer hit the water. Her hair floated upward with a stream of bubbles, and she swam her way to the surface. She was laughing as her head bobbed up and down in the waves their bodies had made from the jump.

Jenifer tread water for a moment, her face leaned up and her eyes closed to soak in the sun. She waited for Tate to swim under her and grab her ankles or her hips, like he was fond of doing. He didn't. Jenifer turned in a circle, her arms swishing and the water lapping against her shoulders. Tate hadn't surfaced.

"Tate?" Jenifer asked in a soft voice. "Tate?" she called, louder. Her voice ricocheted off the rocky cliffside and skittered across the water. "Tate!" Jenifer scanned the clear water, but she couldn't see him. She kept calling his name and hearing her voice bounce back at her. She swam breaststroke toward where they'd jumped in, her heart beating faster, passing a flailing turtle with fins flapping. She dove under, reaching, praying, until a hand grabbed her ankle, and relief flooded her because Tate was fine, he was just joking, he could hold his breath forever. Until Jenifer met Tate's panicked eyes through the water, and a second hand joined the first, pounding against her skin. Jenifer grabbed Tate by the armpits and swam toward the surface as hard as she could.

Black River Falls, Wisconsin
July 2011

"It's a miracle you didn't drown," Dr. McIntosh said, standing at the foot of Tate's ICU bed. "Wazee's over three hundred feet deep in places. This young lady saved your life."

Jenifer was sitting in a chair beside Tate, both of her hands wrapped around his right fingers and wrist. Tate's wet swimming trunks were in a plastic bag at her feet, and she was shivering in the bikini top and long, white skirt she'd thrown on. The past few hours were a blur of getting Tate to the shoreline, hiking back up to find their belongings and call for help, arriving at the ER by ambulance, Tate getting transferred to the ICU.

Tate hadn't hit his head, and he didn't get disoriented in the water, nor did he break a limb. He'd landed on a rock outcropping sideways. It hit his spine. He couldn't walk. He couldn't feel anything from the waist down.

Tate was silent, staring off into the distance with his fingers loosely wrapped around Jenifer's. His hospital gown slouched off his shoulders awkwardly and wires hung between his arms and chest and an overhead beeping monitor.

"Is he going to be okay?" Jenifer asked Dr. McIntosh.

Dr. McIntosh pressed their mouth into a thin line and looked over at Tate. "We'll take you back for an MRI in a little bit. Just hold tight for now." Dr. McIntosh left the room, leaving Tate and Jenifer alone in the ICU with the automaton heartbeat.

"We'll figure this out," Jenifer said, cupping Tate's face in her hands. "Scott and Linda will be here soon, and the doctor will run those tests, and—"

"Jen, I can't walk," Tate interrupted, staring over Jenifer's shoulder. He was pale, with deep circles under his eyes. "I can't move my legs. I can't feel anything." He rested his head back against the hospital bed. "Jen, I'm—Jen this is—"

"We'll wait for what the doctor says," Jenifer tried to reassure, swiping her thumb over Tate's cheek. "It's only been a few hours." She took a shaky breath. "It'll all be—"

"Jen, we're over."

Jenifer blinked rapidly, her heartbeat doubling in speed. Her thumb stilled on Tate's cheekbone. "What?"

Tate pushed Jenifer's hand away and refused to make eye contact. "We're done. I'm breaking up with you."

"Tate," Jenifer whispered, listening to the beeping of the machine. "Tate, you don't mean that. We'll get through this together, we can face anything together, we—"

"No, we can't. Get out, Jen. Before my parents get here." Tate was staring at the corner of the room, not facing Jenifer.

"You're not making sense."

"Get out!"

Jenifer stood, in a daze, and stumbled toward the door. She turned back to look at Tate, at his hair that had dried in every which direction, at the fresh sunburn on his forehead, at the freckles peeking out from his hospital gown. It didn't feel real. Any of it. Jenifer was tumbling through this surreal, parallel universe. Tate was fine. Tate loved her. Tate was going to marry her.

"Get out, Jen."

Jen did the only thing she could figure to do in that moment. She left.

New York City
July 2011

Jenifer was openly weeping, her head in her hands. She was slumped over on the orange backstage couch, and Lilith was rubbing Jenifer's arm, slowly, shoulder to elbow and back. Where Jenifer's feet were on the floor, spindly vines had broken through. They grew in a lattice up Jenifer's blue sneakers, then around her ankles, and up over her jeans and past her shins.

"And—and—" Jenifer sniffled into her palms. "I don't know why this is all happening. I don't know why

Tate got hurt, or why he pushed me away. This is the longest I've gone without talking to him in four years! I keep calling the hospital and they can't tell me anything about him except that he's there and he's in room 119. Linda won't call me, Tate won't call me, they won't even send a text back. The love of my life might be paralyzed, and no one will tell me anything." The words came out in a rush, punctuated by tears. The vines crawled up to Jenifer's knees.

"Breathe with me," Lilith said. "Breathe in and out." Jenifer listened and the two women sat in the silence of their hushed breaths, their chests rising and falling in sync. Lilith waited for Jenifer's sobs to subside before whispering, "You need to go back to the hospital."

"Tate doesn't want me there. There's nothing I can do—" Jenifer's voice cracked.

"You need to go back there, for you," Lilith said, rubbing Jenifer's arm again. "If you stay away now, you will always ask yourself, 'What if?' You will always wonder what happened and look for answers where there are none. Go back there, one more time, and *fight*. Take the leap of faith."

Jenifer nodded slowly, staring at her feet and the green latticework. "I don't understand why he's reacting this way. I don't understand why he won't talk to me."

"Go ask him."

Jenifer turned to look at Lilith and whispered, "I'm so scared."

"Love is the most exhilarating and terrifying experience there is. Don't let fear stop you, my dear."

"Okay," Jenifer whimpered, weaving her fingers into the vines and tugging on them, pulling them away from her legs until they started fraying. "Okay," she repeated, with more conviction.

"My only parting advice is this: whatever Tate says to you the next time you see him, *believe him.*" Lilith squeezed Jenifer's arm lightly, "Listen to him. Even if he refuses to see you, that is his response. Jump, just one more time. But remember who you're jumping for."

Black River Falls, Wisconsin
July 2011

Jenifer approached ICU room 119 with her heart in her throat. She'd tried calling Linda and Tate to let them know she was coming, but neither picked up her call or replied to her voicemails. Her sneakers squeaked against the hospital hallway floors.

Jenifer knocked before entering, and Tate called out, "Come in." He was alone in the room. He was sitting up, watching a TV in the corner flashing reruns of *Friends*. His hospital gown was still hanging off his shoulders, a trail of freckles disappearing behind the fabric. "Jenifer," Tate said in a low voice. He used a remote to silence the TV. "Jen, what are you doing here?"

"I need to talk to you," Jenifer said. She walked across the tiny ICU room and perched on the edge of a rolling chair, her hands clasped tightly in her lap. "How are you doing?"

Tate raised an eyebrow. "Jen . . ."

"I don't understand!" Jenifer said firmly. "I haven't even wrapped my head around the fact that you're in the *hospital*, let alone that you've, what, broken up with me?" Jenifer lowered her voice and her shoulders hunched inward. "Tate, I am so *confused*."

Tate bit his lip and stared at his lap. He swallowed hard. "Doctor says I'm paralyzed from the waist down. With time, maybe, that could change, but I shouldn't get my hopes up."

"Okay, we'll figure it—"

"No! Jen, there is no 'we' anymore."

"And why not?" Jenifer stared at Tate from where she sat, and Tate kept his gaze downward.

"Jen, this would be you, here in the hospital. The only travel you'd ever get, hospital to home, then stuck somewhere forever. Our life is based on adventure. I can't ask you to—"

"You're the greatest adventure I could ask for."

"Jen—"

"I mean it."

Tate finally met Jenifer's eyes. "I can't ask you to stay," he said softly. "Not with . . . not with how I am now."

"You don't have to ask me to stay. I just will."

"No, you won't, Jen." Tate set his jaw. "This is over."

Jenifer took a deep, shaky breath. "Okay," she said. "Okay. I listened. I did." She looked at Tate in the hospital bed, taking in the sight of his broad shoulders and his ruffled hair and his freckles, one more time. "Goodbye, Tate."

Jenifer barely made it out of the ICU and to the hospital lobby before she started bawling. She plopped down in a waiting room chair and sobbed into her hands, not caring who heard or saw.

"Miss, are you okay?" Jenifer cracked open her clenched eyes to see a middle-aged woman in a wheelchair holding out a tissue. "Miss, do you need a tissue?"

"Oh," Jenifer sniffled, "thank you."

"Of course. Can I sit here, beside you for a moment? My partner is running late." Before Jenifer could respond, the woman backed her wheelchair into the space between Jenifer's chair and the wall. "He's always running late," the woman said. "He can never remember my appointment times."

"I'm sorry," Jenifer said, tears still falling down her cheeks and splattering against her jeans.

"Oh, it's alright. No one is perfect. I'd still pick him every day of the week. Even on weekends, too." The woman smiled softly. "I hope you feel better, whatever ails you."

"Thank you."

The two women sat side by side in silence for a few minutes. Jenifer scrubbed at her tears with the tissue. The woman began humming a lullaby. They watched the hospital lobby swirl with people, a hubbub of running children and the elderly with canes and walkers. Eventually the woman's partner emerged from the crowd, red faced and apologetic. He kissed her on the forehead before they left, out of the lobby, down a hallway and out of sight.

Jenifer pulled out her phone and called Billy. He answered on the first ring. "Hey Billy?" Jenifer asked, "do you think we could go out to the beach, like when we were kids? And find the saltwater taffy?"

"Um," Billy replied, his voice crackling over the line. "I mean, sure. But I don't remember what beach it was, exactly. Oregon coast maybe? Or maybe California?"

"We can ask Mom and Dad where it was."

"Jen, are you alright?"

"No, I'm not. Tate and I are done."

"I'm really sorry."

"Me too."

The two siblings stayed on the line for a few minutes, both breathing into the receiver, neither wanting to hang up quite yet. "I could book the plane tickets to the beach," Jenifer offered. "If you wanted."

"That sounds like an adventure."

The Thunder

Central Avenue
4:23 am.

The two-story, red-brick buildings of Central Avenue glittered in blurry streetlight as raindrops pitter-pattered against flat roofs and rainwater whirred through gutters. The weather lulled listeners with a siren's hum. Currents swum through the marbled cracks of aged sidewalks and along the yellow-painted curbs, embracing flaking paint chips and carrying some away on a whirling adventure through the sewers.

The shops of Central Avenue were closed. Spotlights in the bases of window displays, streetlights, and blinking stoplights coated the pavement and buildings in an opaque glow. Flashes of lightning taunted the mortal lights with power they would never harness. The shop awnings were in blocky letters or cursive letters or bubble letters, but they were all painted letters and did not blink on and off in neon colors like the sign at the gas station down the street. In the night, the shops were navigated by memory.

Taylor's, the boutique that specialized in floral blouses and floral skirts and floral dresses and even floral shoes. The movie theater, family-owned for three generations, with its permeating stench of popcorn grease that clogged the teenage employees' already oily pores. The bank, with a 24/7 ATM outside the metal front doors. *Vanessa's*, an adult sex-store with mannequins wearing cheap lingerie in the window display. Behind the headless mannequins was a blanketed, black background that boarded up the window, refusing a glance inside for curious passersby, keeping the children innocent and forcing the curious to own up to what they wanted and step inside. A pharmacy, beside *Vanessa's*. A bar, beside the pharmacy. A fancy restaurant. An ice cream parlor. A children's museum. A hair salon.

The shops owned the day. The mornings belong to post-school-drop-off stay-at-home moms perusing *Taylor's* and plotting ways to run *Vanessa's* out of business. From shiny midday until after dusk, older couples went out to dinner and younger couples went to the movies. The bar was the final soldier, holding out until 2 am. But now, all the shops were quiet. It was the apartments above the stores that owned the night. The apartments and the sky.

4:24 am. A chorus of gunfire danced among the clouds. Jude startled awake. Beatrice startled awake. Cami and Quinn, and Diane and Jenifer, and Amy and Ruth startled awake.

The Movie Theater

Jude was buried beneath three quilts, two hand-made with cotton polka-dot and striped fabrics and one store-bought with Disney princesses plastered across it. Their faces were faded from being dragged across hardwood floors and worn-down beige carpet for the past decade. The blankets begged to slide to the ground. The oakwood guard rails of Jude's top bunk were the only barrier to their descent. Jude's bedroom, which she shared with her little sister Tammy, who was asleep in the bottom bunk bed, reeked of artificial vanilla and popcorn grease from the movie theater below the apartment. Jude ritualistically sprayed the bedroom and her closet with cheap vanilla perfume in a desperate effort to not be the Popcorn Girl at school.

Jude woke all at once, eyes wide open before the thunder faded from the sky. During the night, her mousy hair had wrapped around her ears and tangled against her pillow as she tossed and turned in her sleep. Jude listened for her sister's breathing, but it remained even and deep.

Jude reached for her phone, which was resting on a white-plastic tray strapped to the bunk bed guardrails. The cherry-red, glossy case had two cracked corners: one from when Jude dropped it off the bunk as she tried to shut off an accidentally set alarm on a Saturday morning and another from when one of the tray straps snapped and sent the phone plummeting to the floor. Jude squinted at the lock screen, at her screensaver of Chuppy, the family pug, and waited for a message from Ronnie to appear. She knew there wouldn't be a message. Nor would there be for another three or four hours.

Jude pulled her quilts over her head to obscure the light from her phone. It wasn't fair she had to share a room with Tammy. Tammy was whiny. She stole Jude's clothes. She pried into Jude's business. She read Jude's robin-egg-blue hardcover diary, back when Jude was still naive enough to write her feelings down in a place where a bothersome, grubby-fingered little sister could steal it. But there were no spare bedrooms in the apartment, so Jude and Tammy were stuck together until

Jude moved away to college. Two and a half years and counting.

The three quilts on Jude's upper bunk were two quilts too many to keep her warm in the weakly air-conditioned apartment. Heat rises. The breath of moviegoers and stifling warmth from projectors rose upward with the popcorn stench during the day. Cooling the theater was the priority, with its steady hum of high-tech air conditioning, and the apartment above gobbled up the cold-air scraps. The nights were miserable, with no more movie theater air conditioning.

But though it was uncomfortable and Jude's skin was continually clammy from her toes to her scalp, Jude kept her two extra quilts. The two extra quilts weren't for the heat. They were for hiding the light of her phone in the middle of the night and to create a physical barrier between her and her sister.

Jude pressed her thumb to the phone home button, and swiped to the photos app, to a folder titled, "Boyfriend <3." She scrolled through the photographs, the ones that Ronnie had sent her over the past four months. His goofy grin with the chipped front tooth from a soccer game a couple years ago. The pet iguana he shared with his sister that he called Messi and his sister called Zayne. When he won the state spelling bee with the word 'handkerchief.' His attempt at a sexy face with pouted lips and scrunched-up eyes. His shirtless photos. Photos of . . . other parts of him. There weren't any pictures of them together. They hadn't met in the real world yet. But they would, soon. They were going to meet next weekend. Ronnie wouldn't cancel this time. Jude was sure of it.

Jude switched over to their DMs. "How was your day, hon?" he'd write every evening. "I wish you were here with me," during his biology class and, "I miss you, hon," around dinner and, "what are you wearing?" at night. "Here is more of me," with a shirtless picture and, "I want to see more of you." When Jude giddily complied, "You're the most beautiful woman I've ever seen."

Jude turned off her phone and stared into the darkness her quilts provided, imagining their first meeting. She couldn't drive yet—she'd only just passed her permit test—but Ronnie could drive. He'd take her to the bluffs in his dad's pickup truck with a ham-sandwich-and-sliced-strawberries-filled picnic basket and fluffy blankets for the truck bed, where they'd watch the stars together and talk about their dreams, how Jude wanted to be a doctor and Ronnie wanted to be a welder, and then he'd kiss her. Her first kiss.

Jude shuffled in her bed, rolling onto her other side, shaking her head to clear the daydream. The popcorn stench curled beneath the quilts.

Maybe their first date could be here, at the theater.

Jude never paid for the movies. She was allowed to enter any theater she wanted—except the ones with the R-rated movies—and slouch down in the last row, onto the scratchy red chairs with a bag of 'borrowed' cherry licorice. Jude once thought this could be a selling point among friends. "Be friends with me and you can go to the movies for free!" At first that strategy worked, until said friends went out for strawberry and chocolate ice cream after the credits rolled and Jude was left behind to clean up their spilled popcorn that had been mashed into the floor tiles by thick-soled Converse.

A movie date with Ronnie would be different. He would try to pay, be a gentleman and hand the dead-eyed teenaged ticket-seller a couple of rumpled ten-dollar bills, then Jude would laugh and drag him away from the ticket booth with a sly, flirtatious smile. They would sit in the back. Ronnie would wait until after the opening trailers to hold Jude's hand, his popcorn-butter fingers rubbing a greasy streak across Jude's knuckles. Jude would have already seen the movie, so that she could watch Ronnie's reactions, watch his dimples deepen or his eyes widen. Or wait, no, Jude would have not watched it. It would be the only movie on the roster she hadn't seen. She would have waited for Ronnie, so that they could watch it for the first time together. And then after the evening concluded, with the popcorn bucket and licorice bag empty, Ronnie would kiss her goodnight. An evening of firsts.

Jude sighed to herself, too loud. Another crack of thunder skittered through the clouds. Tammy stirred in the lower bunk and Jude laid deadly still, her thumb silently caressing one of the cracked corners of her phone case. Tammy stopped fidgeting, and Jude sighed again, quiet this time. She pushed the quilts off her head, checked one last time for a message from Ronnie, and set her phone back on the plastic tray.

Jude drifted back to sleep counting her first-date-kiss daydreams like counting fluffy, unshorn sheep. Six. Seven. Eight.

Taylor's

Beatrice woke groggily, her body startled by the thunder but her mind struggling to piece together coherent thoughts. She had fallen asleep at her desk, atop her schoolbooks. The metal binding of her spiral notebook left painful indents spanning from chin to temple, cutting a ladder of lines across her freckled cheek. Pencil lead from now-smudged algebra problems was smeared across her nose. Her chapter 7 algebra test was propped up beside the notebook, with "52%, see me about a makeup" written at the top in red marker and Beatrice's forgery of her mother's signature in black pen below it.

Beatrice ran her hands through her blonde, curly hair and shuffled to the bathroom to splash water on her face. She couldn't fall asleep again. She had to finish correcting her wrong problems, which she had to turn in before the makeup test. Beatrice glanced at the time on her magenta-pink sports watch, which she hadn't taken off yet. 4:25 am. The makeup test was in six hours.

Maybe Jude could help, Beatrice thought before she could help herself. Jude would be asleep, and Beatrice couldn't ask for help again. Jude would recognize the problems. Algebra 2 with Mr. Anderson was the only class they had together. They sat on opposite sides of the room and never spoke. There was no seating chart, but Jude sat ritualistically front and center. Jude would lean forward in her seat as she took notes. Her head flopped up and down between the blue dry-erase markings on the white board and her purple gel-pen notes. Beatrice sat in the back corner with her friends, Abigail and Sammy, trading gossip and sticks of watermelon bubblegum.

Abigail was cheer team captain. She wore her glossy black hair up in a high tail that swished in time with her blue-pleated skirt as she walked. Abigail was also a beauty blogger. She drew taut lines of brown eyeliner across her monolids and rouged her cheeks with raspberry blush. Her cheekbones glittered with iridescent moondust.

Sammy was the tomboy, the sporty girl who played basketball and volleyball and swam on the swim team. But she was the cute sporty girl, the feminine tomboy kind and hyper-masculine teenaged jocks frequently slid into her DMs. Sammy sauntered through the hallways in floral gym shorts an inch higher than the dress code and her hair smelled of lavender. Except for her athletic uniforms, Sammy never re-wore an outfit. It had to be a full calendar year before Sammy recycled an ensemble, and her bedroom was cluttered with more clothes than a department store warehouse. Beatrice didn't know how Sammy managed to balance athletics, school, outfit planning, and texting seven different boys at the same time.

Beatrice stumbled out of the bathroom and back to her desk. The "52%" bore into her eyes, taunting her. She thought of Jude again. She thought of Abigail and Sammy. Even if they did know the answer, Beatrice couldn't ask them. She would be called a nerd. And not the endearing kind—the greasy-haired and awkward kind.

Huffing, Beatrice snatched up her phone and searched "algebra log x 100 = 2" with fruitless results. She stared absently at her closet, partially zoned out and partially ogling her pink-beaded, ball gown prom dress, which hung from a black hanger. The dress calmed her.

Abigail and Sammy had helped Beatrice pick out the dress three months ago. It was the last time they went shopping together. Beatrice was the only one to get asked to prom by an upperclassman, and a *senior* no less. Her friends weren't so fortunate. Despite Sammy's vast selection of boys, none of them asked her, and those that would have were sophomores, like her. Abigail preferred younger men, and the older boys all knew it.

They didn't waste an elaborate promposal on her. Sammy and Abigail would have to wait until next year for their first prom, but then it wouldn't be the same. They would be upperclassmen in their own right.

David asked Beatrice to go. He'd bought a posterboard from the dollar store, wrote, "It would Bea wonderful if you went to prom with me!!!" in liquid glue, then dumped bottles of gold and silver glitter atop it. He held it up in the cafeteria, right after Beatrice stepped out of the hot lunch line. The glue had run a bit before it dried, so the letters were droopy, and the glitter shed into a puddle on the vinyl tile floor. David gripped the sides of the poster too tight and pushed inward slightly. The posterboard threatened to buckle in the middle.

Beatrice stood wide-mouthed for thirty seconds, reading and rereading and rereading the words. Her gaze flickered between her tray of greasy chicken nuggets, the poster, David's braces smile. And Jude, over David's shoulder.

Jude's eyes were squinted, trying to size up the commotion, then her eyes widened, and she smiled softly to herself. Beatrice wondered if Jude was thinking about Ronnie. Beatrice wondered if Jude wanted to go to prom. Beatrice wondered what dress style would look best on Jude. Not strapless, Jude was too flat chested—not that it was a bad thing!—but an off-the-shoulder with a snug waist would flatter her, a gaudy, plastic-jeweled belt scratchy against her dance partner's hands, or maybe a—

Abigail nudged Beatrice's shoulder. "Say something!" she hissed between clenched teeth.

"I'd love to," Beatrice blurted.

David's shoulders slumped in relief, and he pumped his fist in the air. His friends at the red-plastic cafeteria table ten feet over cheered. "Thanks," David said to Beatrice. "I'll, uh, text you."

"Cool," Beatrice replied as David went over to his boisterous friends and Abigail and Sammy steered Beatrice over to an empty table.

"Congratulations," Abigail said, pushing around a grape on her lunch tray with a plastic spork.

"Yeah, congrats," Sammy agreed.

It was the first time Beatrice had something they didn't.

Beatrice walked across her bedroom, fuzzy-slippered feet sliding across the worn carpet, to run her fingertips across the dress beads. The prom dress was one size too small, but Beatrice wasn't concerned. She had two more weeks to lose the weight, and she'd already lost most of it by running every morning and cutting out lunch. The dress was *the dress*. How could she say no to *the dress*?

Beatrice hurried back to her desk as her phone pinged, the screen lighting up with the message, "Did you hear the thunder?" It was from Sammy. "You should text Popcorn Girl the same thing. Make it some romantic declaration lol." Beatrice stared at the messages, and instead of answering them, she opened her DMs with Jude. Well, the DMs between *Ronnie* and Jude.

The fake account had been easy to make. Almost too easy. Abigail and Sammy helped her, picking a high school a few counties over and following as many of its students as possible, then picking some random dude on the internet and borrowing his photos. The whole thing had been Sammy's idea, but Beatrice was the one who was in charge of the account and responsible for luring Popcorn Girl in. They still hadn't quite figured out the reveal, but when they did, it would be epic.

The first few weeks, Abigail, Sammy, and Beatrice wrote the messages together, before and after school, in the cafeteria, during sleepovers. Sleepovers at Sammy's or Abigail's house, not Beatrice's. They didn't know Beatrice's dad left two months ago or that they lost their 4,000 square foot house or that her mom now worked full-time at *Taylor's* or that Beatrice and her mom moved into the dinky apartment above the floral apparel shop. They didn't know Beatrice lived across the street from Popcorn Girl. Abigail and Sammy would find it all horrifying. Maybe they'd invent a new Ronnie for Beatrice, not that it would work. At least Beatrice still had her silver convertible. Her dad paid it off five months before he took off.

The Ronnie account was on Beatrice's phone only. One night, when Beatrice was struggling with an algebra problem, she asked Jude for help. Beatrice had scribbled the problem out as messy as she could in an imitation of a stereotypical boy's handwriting and sent a picture of it, and Jude had sent back a photograph of neat, orderly handwriting working out the problem step by step. The explanation was perfect. Jude texting back, "We're doing the same homework problems in my algebra class!" was not. Beatrice couldn't ask for math help again, out of fear that Jude would put the pieces together. But after that, Beatrice kept messaging Jude alone about other things, occasionally sending screenshots to Abigail and Sammy for laughs, but otherwise keeping their messages under lock and key.

Abigail and Sammy didn't know about the sexting, or the nudes. Beatrice hadn't told them about it, or the math assistance between sexts. They also didn't know how repulsed Beatrice was searching for dick pics on a private browser. Or how much Jude's photos *didn't* repulse her. How they made her feel the opposite.

Beatrice stared at the messages from Sammy one last time. "Make it some romantic declaration lol," she read and reread. Beatrice clicked off her phone and glanced at her prom dress again to gather her courage, then she dove back into algebra, hoping she'd be done with the corrections by Jude's good-morning text.

Vanessa's

Camilla gasped as she woke, the thunder startling her more than she cared to admit. Max woke to Cami's gasp. "Whatsamatter?" he slurred, reaching for Cami. "Are you okay?" His bright eyes scanned Cami's pallid face. They were lying in bed together, still nude, their waists and legs draped with earl-gray cotton sheets. Fresh love bites speckled their necks and chests.

"I'm okay," Cami yawned. She rolled her shoulders. "Just the thunder." Max settled back down and rubbed his temples with one hand, his palm covering his eyes. Cami admired his chest, humming to herself in satisfaction at both his physique and her handiwork. It was their third night together. They'd met at the bar on Central Avenue a couple of months ago. A one-night stand turned into a second tryst, and now a third.

"Should I head out?" Max asked.

Cami rolled over to check her alarm clock, but it had been knocked to the floor. She stretched a lithe arm out to retrieve it. As her fingernails scraped across the cheap carpet, the pads of her fingers brushed against a pearlescent button. Cami pinched it between her thumb and index finger and squinted at it. It was from the button-down she was wearing earlier, one of her work blouses, which she'd worn to the bar. After a particularly trying day at work, she hadn't bothered to change. It was unlike her to forego an outfit change. And now she'd have to mend the blouse. At least it wasn't one of her favorites.

Quinn, Cami's coworker at the bank downtown, had taken a week of vacation to celebrate her two-year anniversary with her boyfriend. Quinn was probably off at a beach in a frilly tankini sipping margaritas on the rocks and getting proposed to while Cami drowned in a lengthy line of angry customers. No doubt Quinn would come bouncing back into work with a sparkly rock on her ring finger. Some girls had it all.

After deciding to skip the outfit change at the conclusion of her shift, Cami had sauntered two doors down to the bar and ordered two shots of tequila. Max materialized from the crowd as the bartender slid the shot glasses across the counter. He wore a black button-down with only the bottom two buttons fastened. The center of his chest was visible nearly to his belly button and his ochre skin was shadowed in the lackluster light of the bar. "One for me?" Max asked.

Cami knocked back both shots, then grinned. "You can pay for the next round." Two little spots of red lipstick from the corners of Cami's mouth remained on each of the shot glasses.

Max threw his head back and laughed. "Good to see you. Cami, right?"

"Correct," Cami said with a wink. "Max."

The bartender slid two new shot glasses across the counter, and Max picked his up. "You with anyone tonight?"

"I am now." Cami's apartment was the closest, above *Vanessa's*, and the evening took them there after one more round of shots, after six minutes of sloppy kisses, and after the bartender told them to get out. The blouse button must have popped off and rolled under the bed when Max tore her shirt off, right before he picked her up and slammed her against the wall, as he knew she liked. Max was a quick learner.

Cami set the button on the nightstand and pushed it inward so it couldn't get knocked off easily. She'd dredge up the travel sewing kit her mom bought her when she moved in and stitch the button on later. She reached back down for the alarm clock. 4:26 am.

"You can sleep a couple more hours. You've earned it," Cami purred. She set the alarm clock in its rightful place, near the button, and dragged her fingers against Max's bicep. "But you can't stay for breakfast."

"Deal," Max replied, sinking down into the bed. Cami settled down beside him, close enough to feel the warmth of his skin without directly touching him. She faced away from Max, toward the window. She watched lightning flash from behind the tightly closed blinds, then let her gaze settle on the three framed photos resting on the slightly slanted windowsill.

Cami and her mom when Cami graduated high school five years ago, Cami in her black gown and black cap. Cami and her two older brothers on a fishing trip three summers ago, the three of them in worm-embroidered bucket hats and fishing poles with lines cast. Cami and her brothers and her mom when Cami graduated college last year, the crimson tassel of her cap fluttering in the same breeze that tousled her mom's graying hair. That was the last time all four of them had been in the same room together. Cami's graduation party.

Lightning flashed, backlighting the photos and Cami started counting the seconds until the thunder rumbled. She wrapped her arms around her torso and let her gaze fall away from the photographs, to rest on the blank wall opposite her.

Cami would say that her family simply grew apart. Her brothers got married and moved a couple hours away from home in opposite directions. Her mom was still working long hours as a hotel manager despite nearing retirement. And Cami was the dutiful daughter with a fancy bank teller job two states over.

Her family knew nothing about her lifestyle. To the best of their knowledge, Cami had a kind Catholic roommate named Lizzy and together they were the foster moms of a tabby cat named Harold and thirteen succulents, not in a closeted lesbians way but in a best friends waiting for marriage and husbands way. Their apartment was cluttered with sophisticated, spine-bent, classic books but dirty dishes never piled up in the sink. There were never male visitors. The men they were seeing would give them a chaste goodnight kiss at the door.

This was what Cami told her mom over the phone about her life, which her mom then satisfactorily told her brothers. It was a collection of half-truths. Harold existed. Cami rescued him from the dumpster behind the ice cream parlor a couple weeks after she moved in. He was missing his left ear and his right eye. The succulents also existed, but the longer Cami lived in her apartment, the fewer succulents she had. The number of clay pots remained constant at thirteen.

Lizzy also existed, but not in the way Cami described. Lizzy was Cami's second love. For a while they *were* roommates, in a strict definition of the word, meaning Cami once lived in her apartment alone and then she lived in her apartment with someone else. They were totally lesbian—or bisexual in Cami's case—domestic partners that were talking about finding a place with both of their names on the lease.

But that ended. Lizzy wanted Christmases and Thanksgivings and New Years spent with one another's family and Cami just couldn't provide that.

Cami's mom knew none of this and never could. She didn't know about Max or the one-night stands or the nights at the bar or Lizzy or Cami's first love. Hell, she still thought her daughter was a virgin.

She did know about Cami's first kiss, though. Cami was nineteen and in college and it was her first date. She doused herself in vanilla perfume and wore a high-necked, pink-lace, A-line sundress. As her date walked her back to her dorm building, her underarms and upper lip beaded sweat in anticipation. Her date leaned in and gave Cami a quick peck on the lips, then proceeded to never call her again. It had been a pity kiss for the awkward, inexperienced girl. When Cami realized this the following week, she called her mom crying and explained what happened. "The right man is out there, mija," the phone speaker crackled. "You just have to wait."

Now, it had been at least two weeks since Cami had called her mom. She was tired of the half-truths and the secrets and her mom's nagging. Cami glanced from the blank wall over to the assemble-it-yourself desk beneath the window, to the closed laptop with rejection letter after rejection letter from literary agents piling up in her email inbox. She pressed her palms against her burning eyes and as she did, the sky lit up again.

"We should do this again sometime," Max said.

"We'll see," Cami said. She knew they would.

The Pharmacy

Quinn was already sleeping fitfully before the thunder, so it didn't take much to startle her into consciousness. She flung out a hand and grabbed Owen's bare shoulder, but he kept snoring. They were in bed, with Quinn on the left and Owen on the right. Quinn retracted her hand and hugged herself. She twiddled the hem of her sky-blue sleep shirt between her fingers.

Lightning flickered beyond the drawn bedroom curtains, and as thunder rippled across the sky, Quinn knew she wouldn't be able to fall back asleep. She crept to the beach-themed ensuite bathroom—per Quinn's request, though Owen hated it, and last week Quinn had put out an order for new, modern, non-themed drawer handles, appliances, and linens. She splashed lukewarm water on her face, then rubbed lavender-scented soap into her skin. She scrubbed the suds away, then soothed her pores with cucumber moisturizer.

Quinn tried to persuade Owen into a skincare routine, as he desperately needed one, his face a mixture of dry, flaky skin and irritated pimples. He refused. Quinn bought him man-scented face wash for manly men. She found it in the trash bin and gave up. It wasn't important.

Their two-year anniversary was the day before, and they'd both taken the week off from work—Owen was an accountant, Quinn a bank teller—to go on vacation and celebrate. Until Owen realized he forgot to book a hotel, so it became a stay-at-home vacation, and then Owen had a big project he couldn't miss, so it became a Quinn-stays-at-home and Owen-goes-to-work vacation.

Owen came home early on the day of their anniversary with a bouquet of red roses wrapped in a black ribbon and a pink-and-black shopping bag. Quinn was in the kitchen making shrimp-and-tomato pasta. Owen came up behind her and kissed the back of her neck, and then his hands snaked around her waist to shut off the stove. The bowtie noodles were halfway cooked. "What are you doing?" Quinn asked, reaching to turn the stove back on.

"We can eat later. I got you something." Owen held out the shopping bag, and Quinn peeked inside to find tissue-wrapped black lingerie.

"Oh."

"Don't you want to put it on?"

Quinn was hungry, for food and quality conversation, not sex. But Owen flashed Quinn that grin she could never say no to, and upstairs they went, to do whatever Owen wanted. Quinn thought that because it pleased Owen, it would be enough to please her, too. But it wasn't. For her, it was faked orgasms, abnormal spotting, foundation-covered hickeys, and pretending that this is what she wanted, too.

Quinn dried her face on a seashell-embroidered towel and stared at herself in the bathroom mirror, absently worrying about how much foundation she had left. She might have a new tube tucked in the cabinets beneath the bathroom sink, but she wasn't sure. She didn't want to check.

Quinn's nose wrinkled. Cami probably didn't have these problems. They worked together at the bank downtown, both tellers. Cami stepped into work each day with her blazers and blouses and skirts perfectly hemmed and she never teetered once in her office-appropriate black heels. Quinn's blouses were tent-like and baggy. She had to size up or else the buttons would pull across her breasts. She wore black or beige flats, not trusting herself with heels.

Cami had a beaming smile and would wriggle her hips when she was excited and after work she would pop into her apartment above *Vanessa's*—*Vanessa's* of all places, a store Quinn was terrified to step foot into—and change into something slinky, then go to the bar downtown or Uber to a club. Cami must not have to worry about faked orgasms or whether she's pretty enough.

Quinn bunched her hair up and looped a fraying scrunchie around it. With her hair drawn up, more of her bespeckled neck was visible. She'd fix it after Owen went to work. If Quinn put foundation on now, Owen would just try to rub it off to see his handiwork then maybe add more nibbles before he walked out the door.

Quinn crept out of the sea-themed bathroom, past Owen and his snores, and downstairs to the kitchen. The half-cooked noodles were still on the stove.

Taylor's

Diane jolted awake and threw her right arm out onto the empty bed beside her. Her palm patted the flat cream sheets, and she nudged around the bunched-up top sheet. Diane pulled her skeletal arm into her chest and rolled onto her back, staring at the drywall ceiling. She still wasn't used to being alone. It was easy to forget.

Diane listened to the rain pounding against the window. The glass was blurred from age and the rainwater leaking from the faulty gutter above it. Her work uniform—the only clothing items she had bought in two months, purchased with her employee discount—hung from a clear-plastic hanger looped over the open closet doors. Blue-denim skinny jeans. Floral blouse.

Thunder rumbled again, but different this time. Closer. Except it wasn't thunder at all. It was footsteps, then a closed bathroom door, then footsteps again. It was Diane's daughter, Beatrice. The thunder must have woken her, too.

Diane sat up in bed, swung her legs aside and let her bare feet rest atop the beige carpet. The mother in her told her to get up, to check on Beatrice, to make her daughter tea. It's what she would have done before. But now, the overtime employee in her said to tuck her feet back under the sheets and rest her head back on the pillow.

Diane listened to her exhaustion. Beatrice was old enough to take care of herself.

Diane, now snuggled back in bed, laid on her side and counted her blessings. That's what her therapist had told her to do, back when Diane could still afford the therapy sessions. Whenever Diane was drowning in self-hatred or doubt or unable to get out of bed, she had to count her blessings, what she had to live for.

First and forevermore always had been her family, her daughter and her husband, Beatrice and Tony. Diane still forgot sometimes that Tony was not her family anymore, that he left. She had gotten better about it.

Diane's first blessing: Beatrice, her kind and beautiful and hardworking Beatrice who did the dishes without being asked and who had the voice of an angel. When Tony left, Beatrice didn't complain once about the move or the apartment. She simply said, "We'll be okay, Mom."

Diane bit her lip, suddenly counting all the ways she was a terrible mother. She coddled her baby girl too much before, and now she ignored her baby girl too much. Beatrice had been glued to her phone recently, probably talking to a boyfriend she wouldn't tell Diane about, and Diane had planned to give her 'the talk' a month ago, and then two weeks ago, and now she still hadn't given Beatrice 'the talk,' and if her baby girl got knocked up, it would have been because Diane was too neglectful, it would be all her fault, and—

Blessings.

They had a roof over their heads and Diane had a job that could put food on the table. Despite being out of the workforce since before Beatrice was born, a whole sixteen and a half years, Diane was able to get a retail job at *Taylor's* and rent one of the two apartments above it at a discount within two weeks of Tony leaving. The job paid $10 an hour more than minimum wage and the manager was generous with Diane's overtime requests. Money was okay right now. They could cover their bills as long as they stuck to a budget.

Beatrice was still going to school. She drove her silver convertible—the only remnant of her father—to the overstuffed parking lot each day, picked up her friends sometimes, made good grades. Beatrice got a 98% on her last English essay and a 94% on her Chemistry exam. Diane hung the tests on the fridge with rainbow-colored magnets that doubled as chip bag clips.

But even though money was okay right now, that didn't mean they had enough to send Beatrice to college. Tony drained the accounts, took Beatrice's college fund with him, disappeared off the face of the Earth. It didn't matter how well Beatrice did in school, she had to get a prestigious scholarship and financial aid and student loans and—

Blessings.

Diane did not have to worry about the mistress anymore. It had gone on for nearly a year, with the coral lipstick on Tony's shirt collars that Diane had to stain treat and the mysterious payments at jewelry and underwear stores. Diane no longer had to pretend to be in an idyllic marriage. It was a burden she was glad to be rid of.

Except, even though Diane no longer had to hide how she felt, the feelings were still strong as ever. They were found in the rippled cellulite on her thighs and hips. They were woven amongst the streaks of gray in her hair. They were stitched into the designer clothes she wore that she used to afford with Tony's paycheck but now couldn't afford with hers, clothes that used to be too tight but now were too loose as her appetite shrunk linearly with the size of her living space. 4,000 square feet to 800.

Diane swung her legs out of bed once more, but instead of hesitating, she stood. She listened to the swish of her pajama pants' hem against the carpet. A nice, calming tea sounded like a good idea after all.

The Hair Salon

Jenifer had fallen asleep with whitening strips on her teeth. Again. As she startled awake from the thunder and fell off her wooden kitchen chair, she clasped her hands together and raised them to the ceiling. "Thank you, Mother Nature!" she said before scrambling to the bathroom down the hall. She yanked those whitening strips off her teeth and hurled them in the trash can, then slathered her toothbrush with toothpaste and began brushing *very gently* as her gums burned. 30 to 45 minutes, the package read. It'd been at least two hours. She had used a stopwatch instead of a timer, which is why she didn't wake when the 45 minutes were up.

Jenifer spit into the white ceramic sink and leaned over it, flashing a toothy grin into the mirror. Her teeth were a bit translucent. She turned on the faucet and stuck her head under the running water for a drink, her head tilted sideways, allowing for water to pool in her cheek before swishing it around her mouth. Jenifer audibly gasped and flinched backward. She smacked her nose on the faucet while spitting out half the water in her mouth onto the mirror and the floor. It was not her night. No night was ever her night, but this was especially not her night.

Jenifer had struggled with insomnia ever since she started working as a hairdresser roughly a decade ago. She liked to think she was a keeper of secrets, and as such, her brain was functioning at a higher capacity than others, which is why she struggled to fall asleep. The things she knew about that town. The infidelity of husbands and wives, the cheaters at bingo night, the child that won't share their toys at the playground, the unlucky-lucky girl whom the high school quarterback was dating that week. The secrets reminded her of her youth, of her adolescence, of her football-playing high school sweetheart, now in the past. Maybe that's why these secrets rested uneasily in her mind.

Jenifer had been mulling over one of her latest secrets—how poor Diane was skeletal thin after her husband left her—which is why she was still awake at 2 am, which is why she decided it would be a good idea to use the whitening strips. What was the point of insomnia if it let her fall asleep with whitening strips still on her teeth? Now her gums were burning, and her teeth would be hyper-sensitive. Just another thing to keep her awake at night.

Jenifer shuffled out of the bathroom and hovered in the doorway of the bedroom. Her husband, Jeffrey, was asleep in bed. His fluffy pillow poofed up on either side of his head, muffling his ears. He had a stack of half-graded algebra exams on his nightstand. He taught Algebra 1 and 2 at the high school, and his algebra 1 students just had an exam. One of the exams was on his chest, a red pen still in his hand, and the overhead light was on. Jeffrey could sleep through anything. The man was practically narcoleptic.

Jenifer coaxed the pen from Jeffrey's hand and set the exam aside, then snuggled into bed beside him. His chest was warm, even through his worn, sky-blue shirt.

They'd been together eight years. Jenifer was working as one of the stylists at the hair salon on Central Avenue when Jeffrey came in looking for a haircut, saying that one of his friends had scheduled but canceled last-minute and he could take the appointment. Jenifer'd been so brain-boggled by the handsome young man that she picked the wrong razor blade and cut his hair too close to his head. Between apologies and offers to not charge him, Jeffrey said the perfect peace offering would be to go out on a date.

They'd been together ever since, got married three years ago, became Mr. and Mrs. Anderson, then moved into the apartment above the salon together after the current salon owner and previous apartment tenant had one too many kids and didn't have enough room for them all. Jenifer and Jeffrey's romance was magic. Uncomplicated. Simple. Dependable.

But despite all the ways that their life together was wonderful, their apartment was one room too big for them. One bedroom too big. One nursery too big. And no matter how hard they tried, they couldn't seem to have a child to fill up that room with cries, laughter, and dirty diapers.

Jenifer ran her tongue over her too-whitened teeth and took deep breaths. She timed her inhales and exhales with Jeffrey, in and out and in. They stayed there, together, until Jeffrey's alarm clock went off and Jenifer shook him awake three minutes later. The first thing he said was, "Honey, you did your teeth too long again. I'll go get you some numbing oil."

The Children's Museum

Amy woke with tears and stormed out of her bedroom and down the hall. Her dinosaur footie pajamas with the little grips on the bottom didn't muffle her quick footsteps. Her hair was matted and she dragged a canary-yellow blankie halfway down the hallway with her, then dropped it in her haste to get to Ruth's bedroom. "Grammy!" Amy cried, as she clambered onto Ruth's bed and scurried under the red and gold quilt.

"What's wrong, babycake?" Ruth asked blearily, rubbing sleep from her eyes. She pulled the quilt down with her steady crochet hands so she could see Amy's tear-filled eyes.

"The sky is angry. It's going to eat me!" Amy's three-year-old voice was warbled.

"No, the sky isn't angry," Ruth reassured. She rubbed Amy's stomach over the quilt. Her dry skin audibly scratched against the fabric. "She's just a bit sad."

"Why is she sad?" Amy knew what sad meant. It meant ice cream melting off her cone and splattering on the sidewalk on a humid day. It also meant getting a sore throat and an achy head the night before her birthday and Grammy forcing her to stay in bed all day instead of taking her to the zoo to see the zebras. But it could mean other things, too, things that Amy didn't understand yet. Like the pretty wedding ring Grammy wore on a silver chain around her neck. And how Grammy sold her car and when they had to travel further than Central Avenue, they rode the bus. That was somehow sad, too.

"Remember what I told you about mommyanddaddy?" Ruth asked.

Amy thought really hard about it, scrunching up her whole body as she thought it through. Nose tweaked, forehead wrinkled, shoulders tensed, fingers clenched. "That . . . mommyanddaddy are . . . they're . . . they wuv me," she concluded.

Ruth grinned, her smile lines bunching up on her face. "That's true, but do you remember the other thing?"

"No," Amy said quickly. She didn't have the energy to think that hard again.

Ruth pointed at the bedroom window, with its closed, white-slatted blinds, then she pointed up at the beige ceiling. "Mommyanddaddy are up there with the sky."

"Oooh, that's right." Amy's eyes filled with tears again. "The sky is going to eat mommy and daddy!"

"No, no, babycake." Ruth shushed Amy and drew a circle on Amy's stomach with an age-spot-speckled finger. "It means mommyanddaddy are up there giving the sky a hug until she feels better."

"Oh." A rumble of thunder. "I want the mommy photo."

Ruth leaned over to her lilac nightstand and tugged open the drawer. It slid out in intervals, the drawer begging to close and stay closed. Ellie built it fifteen years ago and Ruth didn't have the heart to do anything with it, not to touch up the chipping paint or to oil the drawer.

Inside the nightstand drawer were a Precious Moments Bible, Ruth's jewelry box filled with strings of pearls, emerald earrings and a couple of gold necklaces, a black-shelled flashlight, extra flashlight batteries, and a stack of well-loved photos. The top photo was of Ellie in her military fatigues. She was standing in front of Ruth's old house, the one she had to sell when she took in Amy. The blue shutters framed Ellie's beaming, gap-toothed smile. She was young in the photo, barely twenty-two. In her arms was baby Amy, nearing five months with chubby thighs, a bloated diaper, and fingers in her mouth.

Ruth left the nightstand drawer open, then handed the photo to Amy. Amy collected the photo into her hands gently, as she always did, and tapped her pointer finger against Ellie's face. Then she kissed the photo with a loud, "MmmWhaa."

Ruth didn't know who Amy's father was. Ellie never told her. When Amy asked about her mommy and daddy, it felt wrong to talk about just Ellie, as if Ruth was robbing Amy of something Amy was entitled to but Ruth had no idea how to provide. Ruth talked about mommyanddaddy in a set. Mommyanddaddy love Amy. Mommyanddaddy miss her. Mommyanddaddy are watching over her, even though she can't see them. Children have healthy imaginations, and Ruth figured that an imaginary father figure that Amy conjures in her mind would be better than no father figure at all.

Amy pressed the photo against her chest. The photo crinkled in the middle where it rested against the hem of the quilt. Ruth booped Amy on her button nose with an index finger.

One day, when Amy was old enough, Ruth would tell Amy the truth. Ellie didn't die overseas while serving her country. She died during leave. Ellie was driving Ruth home after an outpatient surgery. Nothing severe, just a benign ganglion cyst removed from Ruth's wrist. The surgery was scheduled around Ellie's leave so that Ellie could drive and wait at the hospital during the operation. Amy was one at the time.

It had just started raining, a foggy sort of drizzling, and the water mixed with the oil on the road, making it slick. Ellie took a turn too fast, and the car just slid. The edge of the road sloped down and the car rolled. Ruth didn't remember anything after that except Amy wailing in the backseat, her little body still strapped into her car seat, the straps digging into her pudgy baby flesh and holding her aloft. She waved her hands and legs in the air, and when Ruth squinted, it was as if she was flying.

Amy handed the photo back to Ruth. "Safe," Amy said. Ruth placed the photo in the nightstand drawer and pushed it closed. Shove. Shove. Shove. Amy's breaths had begun to even.

"You know, we can know how far away mommyand-daddy are," Ruth whispered before Amy fell asleep.

Amy peeked wearily through her droopy eyelids. "Really?"

"MmHm." Ruth booped Amy on the nose again. "Count the seconds between the lightning and the thunder." So they waited for the lightning, and when it glimmered through the blinds, together they counted, "One, two, three, four, five, six, seven, eight."

Off Page
With Attalea Rose
Art by Michael Esparza

Welcome.
I'll be your author today.
So, tell me...
What does the air smell like?

Whenever I'm reading, I can't picture faces.
Sometimes I'll see one defining feature, but that's it.
Characters will speak to me, however, and I'll transpose the story on their behalf.
I don't choose the details, I just listen and write it all down.
In order to finish on time...
I would ignore my family and hole up in my room.
Which I wouldn't recommend.
With Red Rook, the editing process was phenomenal.
The novella would not be where it is without their editing team.
Search in email
Paul <RRP@example.com>
To: Attalea Rose
The novellas came in, you can come pick one up in my office.

It was amazing!
I was flying!
I was at his office seven minutes later.
I was dashing across campus.
He had this big box full of my novellas that he pulled out.
He handed it to me.
It was stunning.
It has a gorgeous cover, and it was very interesting to see the process come together.
I couldn't stop staring at it. Just staring, for hours.

Mocktails

Sparkling pink mocktail

Ingredients:

- pink sparkling grape juice
- strawberry syrup
- lime juice
- lime wheel

Directions:

- In a glass with ice pour 1/2 ounce lime juice and strawberry syrup.
- Fill the rest of the glass with the grape juice
- Garnish with a lime wheel.

Manhattan

Ingredients:

- cranberry juice
- orange juice
- maraschino cherries,
- lemon
- angostura bitters

Directions:

-In a drink shaker add ice, 2 ounces of orange and cranberry juice, 2 dashes of bitters, 1 tsp of lemon juice, and 1 tsp of maraschino cherry juice.

-Shake for 15 seconds and strain drink into cup with 4-5 ice cubes.

-Add two maraschino cherries for garnish.1.

Blueberry Fizz

Ingredients:

- blueberry syrup
- lemon juice
- club soda
- Blueberries

Directions:

-In a glass with ice add 0.5 ounce of blueberry syrup and 0.5 ounce of lemon juice.

-Fill the rest of the glass with club soda.

-Garnish with 2-3 blueberries, and a mint leaf if desired.

Note: to make blueberry syrup put blueberries in a small saucer with 1/3 cup of sugar and 2 tsp of lemon juice. Place on low heat and mix and press blueberries till mostly mushy and a liquid forms. This should take about 30 to 45 minutes. Use a strainer over a small bowl to separate the syrup from the leftover blueberry mush.

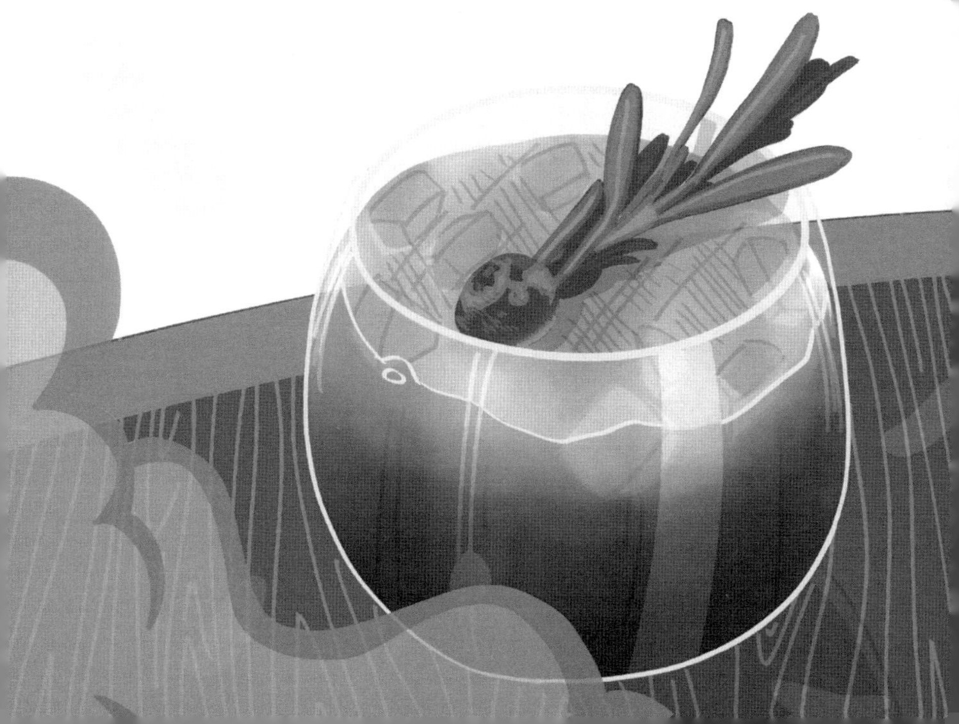

Discussion Questions

• Was there anything in the novella that went differently than you expected? Did you like that it surprised you?

• Which character's story did you relate to or empathize with the most and why?

• How did this book challenge the way you view love and heartbreak in your own life?

• Was there any element of the story that frustrated you? If so, why?

• Throughout the novella, flowers are used to convey different meanings and emotions of the characters or setting. What flower do you think would be best to represent you?

• What do you think you would smell in the lobby of Tranquility?

Acknowledgements

Writing itself is a solitary endeavor, but the process of creating never is. There are countless people along the way that have been instrumental to me as a writer and to this novella, and I'd like to extend my thanks to a few of them.

Thank you immensely to the original Red Rook Press editing team: Abby Armstrong, Anna Kate Baxter, Hailey Drummond, Claire Duke, Hannah French, Camryn Haag, Kelsie Jackson, Cassie Montgomery, and Emma Margret Thompson. Special thanks to Jessica Pelton, the liaison editor, and Dr. Stephanie Marker, the faculty adviser. Without their hard work and dedication, this novella would not be what it is today. Thank you also to Anat Melenteyv and Hailey Drummond for their work on the design and layout of the novella, and to Anat Melenteyv for cover design.

Thank you also to the special edition Red Rook Press editing team: Anna Luis, Quade Mainzer, Toby Monroe, Dylan Melnick, Izzy Piper, Kelsie Jackson, Claire Duke, Martin Albright, Hannah French, Erin See, Camryn Haag, Alyssa Wallner, Alyssa Walker, Abbey Hightower, Hannah Mauck, Olivia LaRose, Lauren Ritz, and Anna Kate Baxter. Special thanks to Cassie Montgomery, the liaison editor, for your hard work and also the incredible person you are.

I am incredibly grateful for my writing communities! Thank you to the members of the Writers' Guild for our Tuesdays of writing together and sharing our work. Thank you to the BBs—Jessica Pelton, Maddie Fries, and Eliza Leicht—for their emotional support and their literary prowess. I am grateful for our coffee dates and steady stream of book recommendations. Thank you to Jessica Wright, Colton Harris, and Tara Bhat, who have listened to me rant about writing projects for as long as I've known them, then have read and given me constructive feedback on said writing projects. Your ideas, criticisms, and support have helped me grow into the writer I am today.

I'd like to extend a huge thank you to the English teachers and professors along the way. Thank you to Katie Hitchcock, who beta-read the first completed book I'd ever written, and for believing in my writing. Thank you to Dr. Brian Whalen for teaching me the importance of idiosyncratic details. Thank you to Paul Albano, who has answered many a 'help, what does this writing/publishing thing mean?!' email from me and has offered continual advice and support.

Thank you to my brothers, the members of the Alpha Rho chapter of Alpha Kappa Psi. Your support has meant the world to me. Ne'er shall I forget my days in Alpha Kappa Psi <3

Thank you to my family. To my mom, Theresa, for being a scribe for my three-year-old self and writing down my stories when I didn't know how to write yet. To my dad, Gordon, for his pragmatic thinking, insistence on triple-checking the publishing contract, and proud-dad support. To my sister, Jo, for complaining about me working on a writing project—namely, this project—instead of spending time with her, not sharing our books with one another, and copying my short stories when we were children (#keepitreal). To my little brother, Walter, my baby, for being you. To my grandparents, Gramma and Pop Pop, for their constant, enduring support.

Thank you to every person that read the original novella. This special edition exists because of you. Thank you for the support, truly.

Finally, above all, always: thanks be to God, and thank you to those that listen.

About the Author

Maureen Edwards—who writes under the pseudonym Attalea Rose—is a fiction writer native to the Pacific Northwest, from the Midwest, and currently residing in the South where she is an accounting student at the University of Alabama. Her short stories appear or are forthcoming in *The Marr's Field Journal, The Albion Review, Arachne Press' Byways Anthology,* and others. She was the contest winner of *Periphery Journal's* 60th issue and the Bumbledeer Award winner of A*udeamus Journal's* Issue XVI. Her debut novella, *When the Flowers Breathe,* was published by Red Rook Press in April 2023. She can be found on Instagram @attalearose.

Red Rook Staff

Red Rook Press is a student-run literary press from the University of Alabama.

Acquisitions

Anna Kate Moorer (liaison), Anna Kate Baxter, Jane Champ-O'Connell, Claire Duke, Hannah French, Camryn Haag, Angie Henle, Aric Huffman, Sydney Jason, Vivian Johnson, Meghen Kellem, Alaina Kelley, McKenzie Knight, Olivia LaRose, Cassie Montgomery, Chance Phillips, Marin Poleshek, Erin See, Jordan Steele, John Underwood, Alyssa Walker, Alyssa Wallner

Audio

McKenzie Knight, Jordan Steele, Ever Wood

Content Editing

Cassie Montgomery (liaison), Martin Albright, Anna Kate Baxter, Claire Duke, Hannah French, Camryn Haag, Aaron Hightower, Kelsie Jackson, Oliva LaRose, Anna Luis, Quade Mainzer, Hannah Mauck, Dylan Melnick, Toby Monroe, Izzy Piper, Lauren Ritz, Erin See, Alyssa Walker, Alyssa Wallner

Design and Production

DeAndra Gauntt (liaison), Angie Henle, Addie Dobereiner, Michael Esparza, Hannah French, Ainsley Greer, Elizabeth Golembiewski, Anna Luis, Jordan Steele, Anna White

Promotions and Outreach

Maya Mungo (liaison), Martin Albright, Anna Kate Baxter, Camryn Haag, Sarah Vance Harrison, Kelsie Jackson, Jordana Kinder, Morinsola Kukoyi, Reese Johnson, Nic Lowery, Hannah Mauck, Cassie Montgomery, Jesse Mullins, Averi O'Brien, Erin See, Jordan Steele

Website Design and Content

Nic Lowery (liaison), Autumn Carpenter, Hayley Green, Aric Huffman, Meghan Kellem, McKenzie Knight, Anna Luis, Jesse Mullins, Ansel Smith, Jordan Steele

Mocktail Team

Aaron Hightower, Olivia LaRose, Michael Esparza (artwork)

Faculty Advisers

Paul Albano, Merrill Lee Girardeau, Stephanie Marker, Jane Morton, Travis Turner